SUNSETS OVER SALCOMBE

Rebecca Paulinyi

For Marie and Jenny, for giving lots of campsite ideas to this non-camper.

CONTENTS

CHAPTER ONE

When Christi had imagined being a grown-up, she had never envisioned being able to reach the oven from her single bed in her box of a flat.

But that was the reality of living in London and not wanting to share her space with someone else.

So instead of shared space, she had no space.

Not that she ever complained to anyone. She had no desire for her colleagues to know that she practically lived in a shoe cupboard. And her parents... Well, she definitely had no intention of telling them. Whenever they came to London, and it was rare, she managed to have some excuse why they could not come to her flat, and instead met them at their hotel. Some of the excuses were bordering on the ridiculous – a bedbug infestation, for one, and a partially collapsed ceiling for another – but she did not think parents had ever cottoned on.

They were generally very busy, and their visits to London were never solely to see her. Both were lawyers, with a thriving practice in the city of Edinburgh, and so their daughter's living arrangements were not at the top of their priority list. That wasn't to say they wouldn't listen, if she wanted to complain. In fact, she was sure they would have offered her some help, quite probably of the financial kind. But she had no desire to be known as the failure of the family. It was bad enough that she knew it was true. No need to acknowledge it out loud.

Christi sighed and began to get ready for work, choosing a smart outfit from her capsule wardrobe. In a flat this size, a capsule wardrobe was the only option. She'd not decorated much, as she had hoped the space would be temporary. But she had hoped that for a few years now. On the fridge, however, she did have several photographs. After all, photos held to the door with a magnet did not feel very permanent. In the centre was a photo of the beautiful Edinburgh Christmas lights, with Christi in the middle, surrounded by her brothers. She couldn't remember who had taken it. She didn't think it was Mum or Dad – they would surely have been working. But the four siblings were beaming, Christmas lights wound around pillars behind them, the streets busy with festive shoppers.

Christi was the youngest of the four King siblings. The youngest, and the least accomplished. She didn't say that – or think it – for pity; it was simply the truth. Her eldest brother, Mark, had left rainy England several years ago on a sports scholarship to a Californian University, and had never looked back. He tried to visit every year, but she couldn't blame him for not always sticking to that. Then there was Logan. He was a doctor, living in Manchester. What parents didn't want to tell the world that their son was a doctor? And Anthony – well, he had followed his parents into the family business. He hadn't joined their firm, but only because he wanted to break out on his own. But he was a fully qualified, and well-paid, lawyer – another of the King successes.

And Christi? She lived in her shoe cupboard, and worked in advertising, and told herself she was happy. And she wasn't *unhappy*. She just wasn't really sure where her life was heading. She certainly wasn't destined for the greatness her brothers had exhibited. And with the way her love life has been going, being a stay-at-home wife and mother wasn't on the cards either. Not that she thought that was particularly what she wanted. In truth, she didn't really know what she wanted – besides perhaps a bit more space, and not having to when the bills came each month about how she was going to pay them.

She shook her head to rid herself of these self-pitying thoughts as she relocated to the bathroom to check how neat her make-up was, having done it in her tiny hand mirror. Her brunette locks tumbled around her face, curling so they didn't quite reach her shoulders. Her eyeliner flicks were pleasingly symmetrical, and she quickly put on a layer of lip gloss before dashing out of the door.

One benefit of her shoe box was it was very central. She could walk to work, and not have to battle on the tube like so many people did. She loved how easy it was to get around London but she hated the stifling heat of the tube, being pressed against other human beings who would not even look at you, the smell of sweat in the air – and quite possibly alcohol, depending on the time.

She arrived with two minutes to get her desk, as she did most mornings, and called good morning to a few of her colleagues while she waited for the computer to warm up. She wasn't really sure how she ended up in advertising. Her degree has been in English, mainly because it was the only subject she enjoyed, and she'd had no idea then what she wanted to do with her life.

Not that she really had an idea now.

Whilst she did not think she was God's gift to the world of advertising, she was confident that she was competent, and she enjoyed working as part of the team, pitching ideas, and seeing the end results. She always felt a spark of pride when her ideas made it into the final project. It was her favourite part of the job.

Christi typed in her password, getting it wrong the first time, having forgotten that HR had made them change them all two weeks earlier, after a possible hacking attempt. It was as her emails were opening that she glanced up and saw Leila walking towards her from the other side of the office, a conspiratorial look on her face.

Christi smiled at her. She was unsure if they could be described as friends, but they went out for a drink every now and again, grabbed a coffee during the day, or sat and ate lunch together.

"Morning," Christi said, more brightly than she felt. She was beginning to wonder if she ever felt as bright as she sounded. How miserable, she thought to herself, pushing it away as Leila perched on the side of the desk.

"Did you hear?" Leila whispered, glancing around the room and then setting her eyes firmly on Christi. There were no hellos or good mornings.

Christi frowned. "Hear what?" she asked. Leila had a flair for the dramatic, and Christi didn't have a clue what she was on about.

"Apparently," Leila said, in a surprisingly loud whisper, "the Thompson contract fell through."

Christi gasped. That actually was quite a big deal. The Thompson contract was at least a quarter of the work that went on in the office.

"How come?" Christi asked, glancing around the room to see if anybody was listening in. Leila's behaviour had made her feel paranoid.

"I don't know," Leila said with a shrug. But that's not the worst part. Apparently they're talking about redundancies."

Christi's eyes widened: redundancies. Never a word you wanted to hear. Suddenly, her concerns about whether this job was what she wanted to do with her life vanished. There were far more immediate worries to deal with. Like how on earth would she pay the rent if she was made redundant? And if Ocean Advertising was making people redundant, what did that mean for jobs in other advertising firms?

At that moment, Mrs Llewellyn came out of her office and gave them both a sharp glare. There was no way she could have heard what they had been talking about, but Leila sitting on the desk was certainly not the sort of behaviour Mrs Llewellyn liked to see. Leila jumped up, and scurried back to her desk. Christi began studiously reading her emails. If they were looking for people to get rid of, she did not want to give them any reasons to choose her.

CHAPTER TWO

The chilly spring was finally giving way to some sunshine, and although Christi was pleased she didn't have to run to work in the rain, her curly hair turning frizzy before she'd even stepped through the doorway, she didn't look forward to the heat of the summer.

In the hot weather, her shoe box of a flat tended to turn into an oven. And there was no escaping it until September rolled around, bringing a blessed autumnal breeze.

Not that the weather was always nice, of course. Summer did not mean a lack of rain. But it did tend to mean a sticky heat that lingered, even when the weather was miserable.

If she'd been lying on a beach with a cocktail in hand, able to cool off in the ocean whenever she liked, then she would have been quite happy about the prospect of warmer weather. But the idea of sitting in her air-conditioned office (if she managed to avoid being laid off, that was) before going home to a warm and claustrophobic flat, was not a pleasant one.

Leila was waiting for her with a coffee when she reached her desk that morning. It seemed to have become a routine, ever since that day two weeks ago when she had told Christi of the impending redundancies.

There hadn't been any, yet, but the rumours still

swirled around. Had Leila decided to be more friendly in some attempt to save her job? Or so that, if one of them ended up leaving, they would have the basis of a friendship already?

Christi didn't know, but she appreciated the coffee and the office gossip that Leila provided. Most of her friends these days were happily coupled up, and so going for a midweek drink wasn't high on their list of priorities.

"Do you fancy a drink tonight?" Leila asked, as though she'd read her mind.

"Yeah, go on then," Christi said. "Just one, though – I can't afford to get drunk, financially or job-wise!"

Leila grinned. "I know the feeling. And then Friday – well, I'll talk to you about that later."

Christi screwed up her forehead. "What about Friday?"

"Just something I wanted to suggest. It'll be better over a drink though."

It was then that Mrs Llewellyn walked in and Leila scurried back to her desk.

While Christi pretended to scroll through her emails, her mind was racing as to what Leila wanted to discuss that needed alcohol to make it easier.

They sat at the bar in the pub down the road from their office. They'd been there together a few times now, as well as with some of their other colleagues. But while the rumours of redundancies had promoted a friendship between Leila and Christi, it seemed to have made the other employees nervous to fraternise.

"So, I'm intrigued what you want to talk about, over a drink," Christi said when their glasses of wine had been pushed in front of them. She always ordered wine. If she ordered anything less strong, she drank it too quickly, and was tempted to purchase another. And that wasn't a good idea for her bank balance, or the dreaded alarm call for work the following day.

"Well," Leila said, a glint in her blue eyes. "I've set you up. On a blind date."

"What?" Christi swallowed her mouthful of wine quickly. "Why would you do that?"

"I've got a mate, he's single, you're single – I think it would be good for you!"

Christi rolled her eyes. "You make me sound as pathetic as my parents think I am."

"No one thinks you're pathetic, Christi," Leila said. "Just chronically single."

"I've been out with guys!"

"This year?"

"Well…" She didn't know what to say. There hadn't been anyone this year, Leila was right. All Christi could say in her defence was that she had tried online dating, and hadn't found anyone appealing. And she just didn't seem capable of hitting it off with a guy in a nightclub or a bar and having anything more than a one-night stand with him. And at this point in her life, she wanted more than that.

She just wasn't sure how to get it.

"It's one date, Christi," Leila said. "A nice meal, a chat, maybe a kiss at the end of the night. If you don't like him, I promise I won't go on about it again."

Christi sighed. "He's not someone you've dated and cast off, is he?"

"No! A friend of my brother's. He's in finance, he's about your age too."

Christi squinted. "And how old is that?"

"Thirty I think. Maybe thirty-two."

"I'm twenty-eight!" Christi exclaimed, feeling slightly annoyed. It was only two years, but thirty felt a hell of a lot older than twenty-eight. Being in her late twenties with no idea where here life was going was far less depressing than the same situation at thirty.

She agreed in the end because she had no reason not to. She only hoped he didn't take her somewhere fancy and then ask her to split the bill, because that would be enough to make her rent tight for the month.

She was sick of never having enough money despite earning fairly well. The rent on her flat already wiped her out every month.

Leila had texted her where to meet him, and Christi's heart dropped at the sight of the expensive-looking Italian when she spotted it across the road. She often wondered what use it was to live in London when she could so rarely afford to do anything in London, but now was not the time to lament her lack of money. Perhaps she would just have to tell him, up front, that she couldn't afford to split the bill.

How embarrassing.

She entered the restaurant, glancing around to try to work out who her date was. She ought to have asked Leila for a photo.

She ought to have said no.

Her stomach churned as she looked for a man who was alone, and perhaps looking as awkward as she was. She didn't even know what name the table was under. She wasn't very good at blind dates, apparently.

Either that, or Leila wasn't very good at arranging them.

There was only one man sitting alone, and he wasn't looking around. She wished he was. That would have made it easier to know whether he was the right man. The maître d' approached, and Christi took a deep breath and forced a smile on her face.

"Good evening," she said, pulling herself up to her full, if rather diminutive, height. She had worn heels for the occasion, hoping to give herself a confidence boost.

"My name is Christi King. I'm supposed to be meeting someone here." She only hoped the maître d' had a better idea of who she was meeting than she did.

He smiled and glanced down at the reservation book in front of him. "Your dining companion has already been seated, Miss King. Allow me to show you to the table."

Christi nodded and followed him, well aware of her heels clacking on the hard floor. She did not like how nervous she felt. Why was she putting herself through this unnecessary torture?

CHAPTER THREE

The table they stopped at was indeed the one she had suspected. The only lone man in the restaurant, although without any sign of nervousness that she would have expected from someone on a blind date.

"Your table, Miss King," the maître d' said, and the gentleman sat there – with a head full of thick, dark hair – finally turned around. He smiled, showing a mouthful of perfectly straight white teeth, and leant in to kiss her on the cheek. "Christine, isn't it?" he said, pulling out her chair for her. "I'm Leonard."

Christi forced another smile "Yes. Well – everyone calls me Christi. It's nice to meet you. I hope you haven't been waiting long." She was well aware that she was babbling but she couldn't seem to stop.

"Not too long, no," he said. He flashed another smile, which reminded her unnervingly of a shark.

He ordered wine for them both, without asking, but Christi was rather relieved that she did not have to speak. She didn't understand why she felt so tongue-tied, but there seemed to be no fighting it.

"So you work with Leila, yes?" he said, taking a sip of the wine. "In that little advertising firm?"

Christi bristled at the use of the word *little*, although there was no huge love lost between her and her employers. Especially with how keen they were to make redundancies. She took a sip of her wine to temper her mood before responding.

"It's actually the largest advertising company in the south of London," she said. "And yes, I work there with Leila. What do you do?"

Leonard's eyes widened, almost as though he was surprised that she did not know what he did. But all Leila had told her was that she was a friend of her brothers. And maybe she had mentioned finance? But Christi didn't even know what Leila's brother did. She wasn't even sure she had known Leila had a brother, until this date had been set up.

As he began to explain, she appraised him. He was good-looking, there was no denying that. But she had the irritating sense that he knew he was good-looking, and that rather negated the effect.

"I work for Mountbridge and Sons," he said. "As the Vice President of Finance. But I expect a promotion, before the year is out."

It was only later that she realised his surname was Mountbridge, and that his cockiness about the chance of a promotion was probably for good reason.

"Have you lived in London long?" he asked, waving away the waiter. Christi hadn't had a chance to even look at the menu yet, but she cringed at the rude gesture.

"Since I left university," Christi said. "Six…no, seven years. How about you?"

"I've always lived here," he said. "Travelled a bit in my early twenties, but I'm a London boy, through and through. Do you live nearby?"

She nodded but did not elaborate. She didn't think she wanted his opinion on her tiny flat or the questionable area she lived in.

He did not need a question to start discussing his flat – which, of course, had a balcony overlooking the water. She could only imagine how much the rent was there – or, more likely, the mortgage. Or maybe he didn't even need that. How rich was his family? And how well did Leila know him? Christi couldn't help but think less of her friend for setting her up with such a prig.

As she spied the waiter coming back over, his back straight and his eyes fearful, she glanced down at the menu. She didn't want to be rude to Leonard, but she didn't think it fair to send this poor waiter away again. She baulked at the prices, even for the starters. But there was no way her pride would allow her to admit that these prices were well beyond what she could afford. He would surely smirk or laugh or say something that offended her, and then where would she be? No, she would have to suck it up and pay for it, if he wanted to split the bill. And then she'd be eating beans on toast for a month.

Well, if she was going to starve for the month, she would at least have a spectacular meal tonight.

The seafood linguine sounded great. And her eyes wandered to a tiramisu on the dessert menu. She ignored the prices beside them, and wondered if he would want a starter, too. Her stomach rumbled, and she hoped he couldn't hear it. She'd skipped lunch, after the first employee – Tim from accounting – had been made redundant. It had seemed prudent to show absolute dedication to her job, and so she had made sure her project outline had been completed a full day early.

When the waiter approached the table, he turned to Christi. But it was Leonard who spoke. "I'll have the soup to start, followed by the steak, medium rare." He closed his menu and glanced at Christi.

"The same for you?" he asked.

Christi froze. It was absolutely not what she wanted. But she wasn't sure how to say no. Later, she berated herself for being so weak. But in the moment, she bowed to the will of this undoubtedly arrogant man.

"Yes. Thank you." She closed her menu and handed it back to the waiter. Her voice was a squeak that she did not recognise. She had never thought of herself as particularly meek, but this man made her feel downright pathetic.

As he told her about his car, she let her mind wander. She'd never had any interest in cars. And what was the point for anyone in London, anyway? It was almost always faster to jump on the tube, and they charged you a fortune to drive in the city anyway. Not that it seemed like the cost would bother Leonard. In fact, she rather thought he would see it as a point of pride if he spent a crazy amount on getting around.

Why had Leila set her up with this man? Did she truly believe they had something in common? Or did she believe that Christi was so desperate for a man, the man himself didn't really matter? Perhaps she just didn't know him that well. To look at, from a distance, Christi supposed he would seem like an attractive prospect. The problem was once you got close enough to hear him talk...

She would get through tonight, stomach paying half the bill if she must, and then she would never have to see this man again. That was a relief, at least. But sitting here, with this odious man who clearly thought money was the only important thing in life, it was hard to banish the worry she had about the direction of her own life.

She had a job, for now, but it barely covered her

costs. She loved London... But she couldn't afford to do anything in the city. And her dating life, as Leila had so kindly pointed out, was rather pitiful.

But how could she turn all of that around? She certainly didn't want to turn to her family with her financial challenges. That would mean openly admitting that she had not done as well in life as any of her siblings. And that was a hard pill to swallow. She shared genetics with all these people, she had the same upbringing as them – so why were they all leading lives that her parents could brag about, while she was on a date with this man that she never wished to see again?

It was enough to make her want to drown her sorrows in a whole bottle of wine. Although certainly not at the prices in this restaurant.

When the bill came, Christi was rather embarrassed at how little she had listened to Leonard's monologues. But that was what they were: monologues. Had he noticed, or cared, that she had barely spoken a word? It didn't seem like it.

The skittish waiter placed the bill in front of Leonard, and Christi held her breath. She wanted equality. And if she had chosen the restaurant, she would have happily offered to pay half without a second thought. But here... She had to think twice. Was her pride worth her eating supermarket value beans on toast for the rest of the month?

She breathed a sigh of relief when he pulled out a shiny black credit card and placed it on top of the bill without even looking up. Her pulse began to slow as relief washed over her. This was not an experience she wished to repeat.

He held the door for her and hailed a taxi. "Can I

drop you home?" he asked, one hand on the top of the door of the black cab. Did he expect her to go back with him? Or to be invited to hers for the night?

"I'm only round the corner," she said, semi-truthfully. "Thank you, though, for dinner." She had nearly said 'for a lovely evening', but that would very definitely have been a lie.

"Here's my number," he said, handing her a business card. "We should do it again sometime."

She nodded, planning to bin the card the second she could, and as he slipped into the car and sped off down the road, she didn't know if she was relieved or offended that he had not tried to kiss her good night.

She walked alone in the dark back in the direction of her flat, keeping her pace brisk and her eyes to the floor. It wasn't that she felt unsafe, but she never felt particularly confident alone in the city at night. If she hadn't thought he would expect more, she might well have accepted his offer of a lift. But it was not really worth the risk of having to spend more time with him just to feel a little safer for ten minutes.

Did he find her unattractive, she wondered, as she rounded the corner onto her street. She had worn tight black skinny jeans with heels for the occasion, with a shimmery top that she was sure showed off her assets to the best of her abilities. But he had not tried to kiss her.

As she put the key into the door, she mentally shook herself. She had disliked the man immensely. She had not wanted him to kiss her. She was not desperate. So why was she questioning herself over why their awful date had ended without an awkward kiss?

Her whole body relaxed as she stepped over the threshold, closed the door behind her, and slipped off her heels. She was sure she had a cheap bottle of white in the fridge, and tonight it felt very much needed.

CHAPTER FOUR

If Christi thought Friday night was a personal low, it had nothing to how she felt when she woke up Saturday morning – although it was only just still morning, according to the clock on her oven, which she could see from her bed.

Her mouth was dry and her head was pounding when she came to, and she blinked for a few moments, trying to figure out what had woken her, and why she felt so terrible.

The why wasn't too hard to figure out, once she remembered the bottle and a half of wine she had polished off the night before. She wasn't a big drinker, usually, but her misery after the terrible date had got the best of her. She'd sent several drunk texts to Leila, asking what she was thinking – but by the time she had passed out, she had not received a reply.

But the what was momentarily a mystery. She still felt tired. She had nowhere to be. No one would know, or care, if she spent the entire of Saturday in bed.

And then a splash of water hit her head and she jumped up, falling out of bed as she looked up to the ceiling. It was bowing, and water drops were falling through it. Well, that explained why she had woken up.

With an almighty crash the ceiling gave way, covering her bedroom in dust, plaster, and a whole lot of water.

Christi screamed, mostly in shock at how nearly she had been crushed by the falling ceiling. Above her, someone was swearing loudly.

"Are you okay?" the voice called.

Christi was shaking. "I...think so. But my flat..."

"I'm calling for help," the discorporated voice said. "Just get out of the room. The building, maybe. I don't know."

Christi nodded, although the person speaking – who was clearly standing well back from the gaping hole – obviously couldn't see her. Water seeped into her belongings, but there was nothing she could do now. Her pyjama trousers were soaked at the bottom, but she was just grateful her drunk self had had the presence of mind to put on pyjamas the previous night.

She grabbed her phone and slipped from the room, and then exited her flat. On the landing, other tenants were looking out of their doors. They'd clearly heard the screams and the crashing, although it did not seem like anyone else's flat had suddenly become a swimming pool.

The sound of footsteps on the stairs made her turn, and a harassed-looking middle-aged woman ran down the stairs. Christi had no idea what her name was, but she presumed she was her upstairs neighbour.

"Are you okay?" she asked. "I'm so sorry. I've rung the landlord of the building, he's coming over. Was anyone hurt?"

Christi shook her head. "It's just me. My stuff, though..."

"The insurance should cover that," the woman said.

Christi swallowed, remembering with a shudder that she had cancelled her contents insurance, struggling to afford the payments.

"I'm so sorry," she said, running a hand through her hair. "My husband... He doesn't remember... I didn't know the bath was running. Not until..."

Christi swallowed again. She felt in a state of shock. Her hands were cold, her head was whirring. But she could tell this woman was distressed, too. And she had not intended to have the contents of her bath pour into Christi's bedroom.

"It's okay," she said, her voice shaking a little. "It's not your fault."

"Do you have somewhere to go?" the woman asked. "I don't know how long..."

It was noticeable that the doors around them began to close then.

The woman glanced at the stairs, and back at Christi.

"You go," Christi said, running a hand through her knotted curls. "I'll be fine."

She pulled her phone from her pyjama pocket as the woman disappeared upstairs, taking the steps two at a time. It only had ten percent battery left. Of course she hadn't remembered to plug it in.

Hey. Disaster at my flat. Can I come round? I'm literally in my pyjamas.

She hit send, thinking that Leila owed her for the previous night. She sat on the floor, her back against the cold stone wall, her pyjamas growing colder around her calves, and waited for a response and, hopefully, an address she could go to. She wasn't particularly keen on the idea of walking the streets of London in just her pyjamas, but what else could she do? She could only hope Leila had something she could fit into that she could borrow. At least until she had got back into her flat, and figured out what was salvageable.

"Christi, darling, how are you? Is this a good time?" The soothing tones of Aunt Olivia, her mother's older sister, came through the telephone, and Christi smiled in spite of herself. Her aunt generally called once a month, always without warning, and often just when she needed it most.

Leila was in the shower, and Christi was stretched out on the sofa she had been using as a bed for the last two nights, while the damage to her flat was repaired. It was lucky Leila was happy for her to stay, for she couldn't afford a hotel, and she needed to be close enough for work. This was surely a bad time to take unexpected leave.

"Hi, Aunt Olivia," Christi said, settling back into the cushions. "I haven't got too long, I'm afraid, I'm staying at a friend's."

"Oh, that sounds nice! Well, don't let me keep you if you're busy."

"No, no, it's fine, she's showering anyway. And it's not so much a girl's night in as being an unexpected guest," Christi said, filling her aunt in on the damage to her flat, her ruined belongings, and the hope that she would be able to get back in very soon. Surely there was a limit to Leila's hospitality.

"Oh, my dear," Olivia said, sounding genuinely sad. "How awful. You know you're welcome here, any time you like."

Christi smiled to herself. Her aunt was always very generous – but she lived in the middle of nowhere in

Devon, and it certainly was not a realistic place for Christi to live. Great for a holiday, but not for her job in London.

"How are things at the campsite?" she asked. It was always easy to talk with Aunt Olivia. Not like when her parents rang. Then she always felt on edge, waiting for the hidden barb, or the comparisons to her siblings. She wasn't even sure her parents were aware they were doing it. It was just something they couldn't help.

She hadn't told them about the leak in her flat. She would have to, if the repair work went on for too long. She couldn't stay on Leila's sofa forever, and she couldn't afford anywhere else without some help. Her rainy day fund didn't stretch far enough to cover full-on floods.

"Oh, getting ready for the busy season," she said. "I've got Oscar – do you remember him? Oh, probably not. He's lived around here all his life, does landscaping and the like. He's getting the field ready, while I tend to the paperwork. I'm not as young as I once was!"

Christi laughed. "You're forever young, Aunt Olivia."

"Have you heard from your parents lately?" Olivia asked. "That sister of mine is always so hard to get hold of!"

Christi's smile became tight, even though there was no one to see her. "No, not for a few weeks," she said. "And if you do speak to Mum... I'd appreciate you not mentioning about my flat." She paused for a moment. "Don't want to worry them," she added.

"Ah. Of course, dear. It stays between us." Christi always got the sense that Aunt Olivia understood her like no one else did. Perhaps because she had been the hippy older sister, always compared to her high-flying sister. Where Olivia had chosen to buy a campsite and spend her days looking out to sea, her sister Emma had got her law degree, married a lawyer, and had a brood of seemingly perfect children.

And Christi.

"I mean it though, Christi. You're always welcome, here. I'm run off my feet. I could give you a job, somewhere to live, if you wanted it. Might be a nice break from London. And I'd love to have you here."

As gratifying as it was to feel wanted, she couldn't just give up everything and move to Devon, and certainly not just for the summer season. She had a life in London, a job, a flat – well, hopefully she would again soon – and friends. She could spend the summer in Devon, and she would probably be happy. But what would she do after that?

The next day she walked to work with Leila, and hoped that the landlord would be in touch. Not that she checked her phone too obviously during work hours. She didn't want to give them any excuse to make her redundant.

Just after twelve, she felt her phone vibrating in her pocket. She glanced at Leila, who was typing away at her computer, and decided to dash out and take her lunch break, while answering the call. Leila would forgive her for not waiting around.

When she got outside the building and pulled her phone out, it had stopped ringing – but the display told her that rather than the landlord calling, it had been her mother.

She debated calling back as she waited for her toastie at the local coffee shop. If she didn't, the thought of the call would be hanging over her. But if she did, she knew there was a decent chance she would spend the afternoon feeling despondent.

With a sigh, she hit the button to redial, and leant against the wall outside the building as it rang. The spring sunshine had broken through the clouds, and she closed her eyes and soaked in the Vitamin D.

"Hello, Emma King speaking."

Christi was sure her mother had a display to tell her who was ringing, but her answer was always the same.

"Hi, Mum," Christi said. "Sorry, missed your call."

"Christi!" her mum exclaimed, sounding genuinely surprised at the voice on the other end of the line. Christi could picture her buried in a mound of paperwork for her latest case. "I did wonder if you would be at work."

"Just out on my lunch break," she said.

"And how is work going? Any news?"

She couldn't tell her mum about the rumours of redundancies, and she'd certainly not had a promotion or bonus of any kind since they had last spoken.

"It's fine," she said. "Same old, same old. How's your work? And Dad's?"

"Oh, you know us. Always busy. Your brother wanted us to head out to see his game next month, but I just can't see how we'll get the time to get to America!"

"No, that's quite a trip." They barely made it to London with any regularity, so she had no idea how they would find time to go to America.

"Have you spoken with any of your brothers lately?" Mum asked. "I think Logan might be seeing someone, although when I ask outright he just denies it."

"Not in a while," Christi said, screwing her face up and trying to remember when she had last spoken to her brothers. "But I'm sure he'll tell you, when he's ready! I spoke to Aunt Olivia yesterday," she said, feeling like her side of the conversation was rather sparse.

"Oh yes? How is she doing?"

"Well, I think. Busy, start of the season and all. She said she'd like me to go down and help, for the summer!"

Her mother laughed. "Like you can give everything up for two months and then come back like nothing's changed! She lives on another planet, my sister."

And even though Christi had thought something similar herself, she didn't like how dismissive her mother was. "It's beautiful down there," she said.

"Oh, yes, it is. Perfect for a holiday. But not to live. There's nothing there. You're not actually thinking of going, are you, Christi? Your career will be ruined!"

Christi thought of the redundancies looming over the whole company and then pushed the thought from her head. "No, I'm not," she said. "But it was nice of her to ask me to."

"If she wants cheap labour, surely there are uni students down there who want a summer's worth of work."

Christi was fairly sure her aunt hadn't asked her just for cheap labour but, as usual, she didn't push the point. Her parents won arguments for a living. She always ended up exhausted and not quite sure what her point was.

"I'd better run, Mum," she said. "Got to get back to the office." If her mother understood anything, it was being a workaholic.

"Of course. Well, take care – and let me know if you hear anything about Logan's mystery girlfriend!"

Christi closed her eyes for a moment after her mum had hung up. She wished her parents didn't get to her so much. Everything they said put her on edge. There was no way she could go to them, admit that she needed her help. Not when her brothers were all so successful, and never needed to ask for help at all.

She polished off her toastie and headed back inside. She certainly wasn't going to allow the company to fault her timekeeping.

CHAPTER FIVE

It wasn't until two days later that the landlord finally rang, and the news wasn't good.

"They've found asbestos," he said. "The repair job will be huge – there's no way you can move back in for a month at least."

"A month!" Christi exclaimed. "But what am I meant to do?"

"If you can find somewhere to stay, then I won't charge rent for this month, and we can go on as usual after that."

"I don't know where I could stay for a month."

"If you need to give notice, just let me know."

She sighed. "Can I think about it?" she asked. "I'm just going back into work."

"Course. I'll get the work started, either way. Luckily I can claim it on the insurance. And if there's anything else you want out of the flat, I can let you in. You'll have to wear a mask, though. Thanks to the asbestos."

Her mind was a mess that afternoon as she attempted to work. Where was she going to stay? The water had ruined most of her things, and the furniture belonged to the landlord, so she didn't need to worry about that. But there were items around the house that she would definitely want if she wasn't going back for a month.

And maybe not ever.

She couldn't stay on Leila's sofa for a month, and nor could she afford a hotel. So perhaps her only choice was to find somewhere new, give notice on her flat and start over. She could barely afford the rent as it was. Would it be possible to find something else nearby that she could manage the rent on by herself?

Adult life was far harder than she had ever imagined. Leila glanced over at her several times, but Christi wasn't ready to share yet. She needed to have a plan, first, before she told anyone that she was homeless for at least a month.

And then, at a quarter to four, Mrs Llewellyn came out of her office. She walked straight up to Christi, stopped at her desk, and smiled.

Christi's heart froze. Mrs Llewellyn never smiled.

"Could you pop into my office for a moment please, Christi."

Feeling like there was lead in her feet, Christi pushed her chair back and stood up. She was sure everyone in the office was watching her. After all, had she not stopped and watched the others, when they had been called into the office?

She hoped as hard as she could that this wasn't what she thought it was... But what else could it be? Mrs Llewellyn never called her into her office. She liked to keep herself separate from the rest of the minions.

She closed the door, and indicated a black plastic chair in front of her desk.

Should she start begging for her job, Christi wondered to herself. Tell Mrs Llewellyn that she had just been told she had no home, surely she could not have her job taken away on the same day?

But her tongue seemed to be frozen.

"Christi," Mrs Llewellyn said, looking at her over her spectacles. "I am sure you have heard of the challenges facing the company, and the response the company has been forced to make."

Christi swallowed. "Redundancies," she said, her voice sounding hoarse.

Mrs Llewellyn shuffled the papers on her desk and did not make eye contact.

"Yes. I'm afraid so. And while Ocean Advertising is very sad to have to let people go, it cannot be avoided. I'm sorry to say we have no choice but to make you redundant, Christi. Effective immediately."

Mrs Llewellyn began to talk about a redundancy package, but Christi couldn't focus. Her mouth had gone dry and her mind blank. It was impossible to comprehend that this could be happening – let alone on the same day that she found out she was effectively homeless.

"Do you have any questions, Christi?" Mrs Llewellyn asked. Christi blinked. From the way the older woman was staring, Christi didn't think it was the first time the question had been asked.

"Do I... Go now?" she asked.

"In the circumstances, there's no need for you to work until the end of the day," she said. "We do wish you the very best of luck, Christi."

Christi nodded, her head buzzing, and walked to her desk in a daze. She didn't have much to empty from it. A few coins from her lunch, a notebook and pen, and her phone charger. The rest belonged to the company.

She could feel Leila's eyes on her, and when she eventually looked up, her friend's eyes were wide.

Tears welled in Christi's eyes and she simply nodded, confirming Leila's suspicions.

"No!" Leila mouthed.

Christi took a deep, shuddering breath and decided to exit the building before she burst into tears. Leila needed to stay until five, at least, and she would tell her all about it that night. After all, she had nowhere else to go.

She stopped at the shop on the corner of the road and picked up a bottle of wine. She was on her way to the counter when she decided that would definitely not be enough and turned to pick up another. Tomorrow she would have to face the fact that she needed to find a job and a home, but tonight she planned to drink with Leila and forget all about it.

But Leila wouldn't be home for a while, and she couldn't sit with her thoughts. Once she got back to Leila's flat she opened the first bottle, not caring that it hadn't been chilled, and poured a large glass. It was warm and a dryer white wine than she usually drank, but she took a large glug, and then rifled in the freezer, pleasantly surprised that Leila had a tray of ice cubes in there.

Never before had she felt so alone. She couldn't ring her parents, or her brothers. This was too humiliating to admit. She could ring Aunt Olivia... but they had only spoken recently, and it would be out of character for her to ring again so soon. Especially since she had turned down her aunt's offer.

Tears rolled down her face as she drank the wine, hoping it would numb her sadness a little before Leila returned home.

Leila burst through the door just after five o'clock.

Christi was well into her second glass of wine, and the tears had dried up, leaving her feeling empty and miserable.

"Christi! What the hell happened?" Leila asked, throwing her bag down. "Did they make you redundant? Just like that?"

Christi took a sip of wine and nodded. "Just like that. No need to work until the end of the day."

"It's not acceptable. They can't just decide-"

Christi laughed with no humour. "They can, though, can't they. They're in charge."

"What will you do?" Leila asked, sitting down on the armchair opposite her.

"There's some redundancy pay, because I've been there a few years," she said. "So I guess that will keep me going while I job hunt."

"And your flat?" Leila asked.

Christi groaned. "Don't ask. I promise, I will get out of your way soon."

Leila reached over and squeezed her hand. "You know that's not why I'm asking."

"Do you want some wine? I got two bottles, thought one might not be enough."

Leila smiled. "Definitely.

They drank, and cursed their bosses, and did impressions of Mrs Llewellyn, and drank some more. At one in the morning, Leila went to bed, since she still did have a job to go to the next day. But Christi poured herself another glass of wine and watched the traffic out of the living room window. It was mainly taxis, and the yellow lights on their roofs seemed to blur as she drank more wine, mixing in with the red and white lights around them.

What was she going to do?

One option kept coming back to her. The only option she really had.

She could go and stay with Aunt Olivia for the summer. She'd have a job, and a roof over her head. And she could save her redundancy pay, and still apply for new jobs. They surely had internet down in the middle of nowhere in Devon. She could do remote interviews. If she had to pay rent in London, her redundancy money would be gone in no time. And she didn't want to keep trespassing on Leila's kindness.

Aunt Olivia was family. She always seemed to care what Christi was doing. And she wouldn't judge her like the rest of her family would. Her parents wouldn't like it… But she didn't need to tell them the reasons. She could pretend it was all because she wanted to spend the summer in Devon. Be the free spirit her parents always accused her of being. No need for them to know that it was the only option open to her.

It would be nice to spend some decent time with Aunt Olivia, and to not feel stressed and on edge like she did currently. And the space… She hadn't been down there in a long time, but her memories were of a large house and rolling fields. It would be nice to not feel cramped for a little while. And she would surely miss London, and be grateful to come back – even if it was to another shoe box.

The job would surely pay far less than her old salary, but it was better than nothing. And her living expenses would be reduced to barely anything at all.

Before she could change her mind, she pulled out her phone. It was the middle of the night, and her eyes were blurring, but she managed to type out a text message that she hoped was legible.

If the offer of a job over the summer is still there, I'd love to take it. X

The reply was almost immediate, and despite being drunk, Christi wondered what her aunt was doing up at such an early hour.

Of course! I'd love to have you, for as long as you can spare. Just tell me the date and time of the train you're getting and I'll be there to pick you up. Xxx

Christi held the warmth of that message close as she lay down and let the alcoholic haze send her into an uneasy sleep.

CHAPTER SIX

It all happened rather quickly, after that. There didn't seem to be much point in delaying, not once she decided that she was heading down to Devon for the summer.

The day after she was made redundant, she had the worst hangover of her life. She didn't wake up until long after Leila had left, but she didn't want to sit around and think about things. That was a surefire path to misery. Instead, she made herself a strong cup of coffee, took some paracetamol, and tried to make plans.

By the end of the day she had thrown up twice, but she had tickets booked on the train to Totnes for two days later. There was no point in hanging around, really. She already felt bad enough for sleeping on Leila's sofa for so long. Besides, it would be nice to be in Aunt Olivia's comforting presence, when everything seemed so bleak.

She waited until the day after the horrendous hangover to ring her landlord. She didn't think she was in any fit state to speak to anyone the day before – except for Leila, who had looked rather worse for wear herself when she had got home from work.

"Can you keep me up-to-date on the repairs at the flat?" she asked. "I don't want to give you notice, but I might be gone a little over a month."

"To be honest, I think the repairs might take more than a month," the landlord said at the end of the line, sighing. "Shall I just keep in touch, and we can go from there? It's all a bit of a nightmare, to be honest."

Leila felt sorry for her landlord, but she didn't really have much sympathy in her. Her own desperate situation was all-consuming.

"Can I come in tomorrow, and get my stuff? Anything that's not ruined, that is. I'm leaving London for a few weeks."

And so, two days later, Christi was struggling to wheel two large suitcases through London Paddington. The station was busy, as it always was, and commuters dashed around with cups of coffee precariously in one hand, and phones glued to ears. She didn't like travelling with so much, but what else was she to do with it? These two suitcases held nearly everything that she owned. Well, except for the kitchen equipment. That she had gratefully left Leila. She didn't really think she needed to turn up at Aunt Olivia's with a set of saucepans.

The platform was finally announced and she battled through the ticket gates, cursing at one of her suitcases for getting stuck halfway through. No one tried to help, and she supposed she couldn't blame them. She wouldn't have wanted to talk to strangers, either. She wished she'd been able to get a coffee for the journey, but there was no way she could handle one with the two suitcases. She only hoped she would be able to get on board.

Double-checking that the train was indeed going to the little town of Totnes, she found a seat and waited for the train to pull in. She vaguely remembered the train station from the last time she visited. It was tiny; certainly nothing like London Paddington. But at least there was no chance of her missing Aunt Olivia, who had promised pick up.

Christi had offered to get a bus, and Aunt Olivia had just laughed. In the time since she had last visited, Christi had forgotten how sporadic public transport was in the country. She hoped she would manage all right without being able to drive. Having lived in cities all her life, there had just never been any reason to learn.

"The nine fifty-two to Penzance is now approaching platform three. Platform three for the nine fifty-two to Penzance."

She stood immediately, even though the train was not yet in sight. Anxiety and excitement warred in her stomach, making her feel a little queasy. Was this harebrained plan ridiculous? She hadn't got up the courage to tell her parents yet. Not that she generally told them everything, but she would at least mention that they could find her in Devon if they needed her. She already knew they wouldn't approve, but then she didn't think they approved of much in her life.

With a loud hiss, the train pulled into the platform. It took up the whole length, with at least eight coaches, and Christi scanned the signs to find coach C. She had a seat booked, and she certainly did not want to end up standing for this long journey.

She waited patiently for the passengers to get off, and then dragged her suitcases up the step. She was slightly nervous that she would slip and get her foot caught in the gap between the train and the platform. When she managed to get on, she struggled to get down the narrow aisles. Her seat was mercifully empty, but finding room on a luggage rack was more of a challenge. By the time she sat down, she was exhausted, stressed, and in need of a hot cup of coffee.

It took a long time for her to relax into the journey. She kept checking to make sure she could still spy her suitcases, filled with her worldly belongings. And then, when the food cart finally came through, she ordered herself a coffee and a muffin and tried to read a book. But her mind wouldn't focus. So much had changed in such a short space of time, and she felt like she was on ever-changing sands. She hadn't loved her job, or her flat, but they were hers. Constants in her life day in, day out. And now, for however long, both were gone.

She felt too old to be upping sticks with two suitcases containing everything she owned, but there she was. It was only for the summer, she told herself. And there was nothing wrong with being a free spirit.

Except, in her heart, she wasn't sure that she *was* a free spirit. She liked knowing where she would be and what she would be doing. This big change made her feel anxious.

The train had quietened down as they had got further towards Devon, and she was pleased to have had the seat next to her free for most of the journey. She sat in the window seat and watched as the world whizzed by. The fields she passed were green and lush, and then opened out to sparkling waters. She took a deep breath and felt her whole body relaxing. The sea stretched into the distance and it was beautiful to look out over. The sun reflected off it, making it sparkle, and the waves bobbed in the spring breeze. It made her realise how long it had been since she had seen the sea properly, and even longer since she had swum in it. It would be lovely to spend the summer in a place by the sea. Yes, she would be working, but in her time off she could be outdoors as much as she liked. She only hoped they would have a long, hot summer that she could truly appreciate.

She checked the map on her phone to try to work out how far away they were. She wanted to be ready when they approached, since her cases would take some wrangling to get down from the rack she'd wedged them in.

At Exeter, the train suddenly became crowded again, and a middle-aged woman took the seat next to Christi. She tried not to look annoyed. The seat had been free for most of the journey and there was no reason this woman shouldn't sit in it.

Christi forced a smile on her face as she caught the woman's eye. She had short, dark hair with streaks of grey through it, and carried a novel in one hand. Christi couldn't see the title, but she was intrigued by the cover.

"Are you going far?" the woman asked.

Christi shook her head. "Totnes. So I'll get up soon, try to find my cases."

"They never stop long, do they!" she said with a laugh. "Are you going on holiday? Lovely part of the world, Devon. Although I'm going all the way to Penzance, to see my son."

Although she wasn't really in the mood to talk, she didn't want to seem rude. "I'm staying with my aunt, over the summer," she told the woman. "To help her with her campsite."

"Oh, how wonderful. Where abouts is it? I've stayed in a few in Devon myself!"

"It's not too far from Kingsbridge, I think," she said, trying to remember the name. "I think the nearest place is Salcombe."

"Don't think I've stayed there, but I know Salcombe well. You'll have a wonderful summer, I'm sure."

"I hope so!" Christi said. She glanced down at her phone. "I think I'd better get out, now," she said. "But I hope you have a lovely time with your son."

CHAPTER SEVEN

As the train pulled into the little station, Christi was ready next to the doors. She had bumped her head trying to get the biggest of her cases out, and she hoped it wouldn't leave a bruise. She looked out of the window, hoping to catch a glimpse of Aunt Olivia, but the train was moving too fast. There weren't many people waiting to get on, and when the doors slowly opened, only a few disembarked. Christi tried to lift her case, but it threatened to overbalance her and she had to let go of the other to put her hand out and steady herself.

A man in his forties wearing a dark polo shirt jumped forwards and grabbed the first case from her. Her instinct was to keep hold of it, but then he smiled. "Let me," he said, and lifted it from the train, wheeling it to the white picket fence that separated the car park from the platform.

Christi managed the other case by herself, and thanked him, feeling a bit breathless from the near-fall. He got on the train, which departed almost immediately, and Christi balanced her cases and shielded her eyes from the sun, looking for Aunt Olivia.

Her heart felt warm when she spotted her, hurrying down the platform in a dress covered in sunflowers, a wide smile on her face.

"Christi!" she called with a wave, and Christi

grabbed hold of both cases and began wheeling them down the platform to meet her aunt.

They embraced, the suitcases somewhat in the way, and in her aunt's arms, Christi was embarrassed to find tears springing to her eyes.

When Aunt Olivia pulled away, concern shadowed across her blue eyes.

"It's lovely to see you, Aunt Olivia," Christi said, hoping the tears would dry up without her having to explain them.

Olivia took one of the cases from her. "What's wrong, love?" she asked softly.

"Everything's just been a bit too much, that's all," Christi said, forcing a smile. "I am really grateful to you for having me for the summer. I can't wait to see the campsite, it's been years since I saw it. It was just a field then! It's exciting it's so busy."

Aunt Olivia shifted her gaze and began to roll the case towards the exit. "I'm delighted to have you here, love. Although I'm sorry things are so stressful. Why don't you tell me all about it over a nice cup of tea once we're home. I'm sure it's not as bad as all that, really."

It had been a long time since Christi had been a passenger on such windy roads, and her stomach churned a little every time they turned a tight corner. Some of the roads didn't even look wide enough for two cars to pass, and she wondered how Aunt Olivia drove with such confidence. But then, her car was tiny. For several minutes they had not thought they would be able to bring both suitcases with them, since the boot wouldn't close – but they eventually managed to get the back seats down and ram them in.

It seemed to take an age to get to the house, and Christi sank gratefully into a kitchen chair. Aunt Olivia filled the kettle – an old-fashioned cast-iron one that sat on the range cooker and whistled when it was ready. It seemed entirely impractical, and yet suited the place, and Aunt Olivia, perfectly. Christi watched her prepare the tea. Her long hair was entirely grey now, and she wore it in two plaits down the side of her head. Her dress swished around her legs as she moved and pulled out two mugs, one that simply said 'Devon' on it with a green and black flag, and another with an intricate floral design.

"Sugar?" she asked.

Christi shook her head. "Just milk, thanks." She hated the taste of sugar in tea. It made it undrinkable, in her opinion – but she supposed everyone was different. And she didn't mind it too much in coffee.

Soon the steaming mugs were on the large farmhouse table, and a plate of biscuits joined them. They looked homemade, and Christi tried to remember if Aunt Olivia was into baking.

"So," Aunt Olivia said, a kind smile on her face. She had dimples when she smiled, and her blue eyes lit up. "Do you want to tell me what's been going on at home?"

So she told her everything. The roof of the flat coming down on her, and nearly crushing her. The damage to the ceiling, the fact that there was asbestos, and that the whole thing would take weeks, if not months, to fix. The redundancy. That was the hardest bit to discuss, because her aunt had no idea about it. Aunt Olivia gasped, and offered her sympathies, but Christi found she was on a roll now. She told her that her flat was so small she felt claustrophobic in it. That she had never shown her parents where she lived, for fear of judgement. That she was sick and tired of being compared to her brothers every time they came up in conversation.

"I'm sure your brothers don't mean–" Aunt Olivia began.

"It's not them though, is it. I don't even think Mum and Dad realise they're doing it. But who wouldn't be proud? Lawyer, doctor, a top athlete... And then there's me. Working in advertising because it was the first thing I ended up doing when I left university. Well, not even working at that anymore."

She put her head in her hands. "I'm a total failure. They have every right to compare me poorly with Anthony, Logan, and Mark. What have I done with my life? Nothing. Nothing at all." She grabbed a chocolate chip cookie from the plate on the table and bit into it bitterly.

"You can't think like that, Christi. And your parents – yes, they have high standards. And I agree, they are not the most tactful of people. Believe me, I know a thing or two about being seen as the failure of the family."

"I don't think–" Christi began.

Aunt Olivia tutted. "My sister is a lawyer, Christi, married to another lawyer, with four very intelligent, successful children. No, I won't hear any arguing on that score. I, on the other hand, decided to buy a patch of land in Devon, never married, and never had any children. I can assure you that my family has often seen me as the failure."

Christi didn't disagree, because, sadly, she thought Aunt Olivia was probably right. Based on what they thought was important, they probably did see her as a failure. "You're the only one I feel I can talk to," Christi said in a soft voice. "Mum and Dad don't even know I'm here yet. And they know nothing about the job, or the flat. And I'm not planning to tell them."

Aunt Olivia squeezed her hand. "You have to tell them you're here. But the rest of it, we can keep between us. I don't ever want you thinking you're a failure, Christi. If you're not happy with your life, then you should change it. I'm a big believer in making your own destiny. You are not worth any less than your brothers, mark my words."

Christi squeezed Aunt Olivia's hand back, and gave her a watery smile. "Thank you. And thank you for asking me to stay. I was at my wits' end, to be honest. Everything seemed to go wrong at once. Although…" She swallowed, and glanced out of the window at the rather empty camping field. "Are you sure you actually need my help?"

CHAPTER EIGHT

Christi didn't miss the way her aunt's eyes flicked away at the question, or how she began drinking her tea very quickly. "Of course I do," she said when she had swallowed the mouthful of hot liquid. "I was going to hire someone, if you hadn't decided to come. The season's not started yet."

"You mentioned improvements…"

"The toilets are new," Aunt Olivia said, and Christi couldn't help but frown at the dilapidated toilet block she could see in the distance.

"The toilets themselves," Aunt Olivia added. "Not the building. I've got other things in the works it's just, you know, time, money…" She shrugged.

"I'm not criticising," Christi said quickly. "I just don't want you to offer me a job when you don't need me, and if you can't afford to pay me. I know my life is a mess, but you don't need to jump in and save me."

"I'm not jumping in and saving you," Aunt Olivia said. "I didn't even know everything that was going on when I offered for you to come down. I do need your help, I promise, even if it's not as busy as I would like. And let me worry about paying you, please."

"If you don't need me, please just tell me. I'll happily stay here for the summer, if you'll have me, even if there isn't a job." She wondered if her aunt was lonely. Christi knew that she herself was, and she was surrounded by far more people normally than her aunt was. She needed somewhere to live, anyway – and she was quite keen on the idea of a summer in Devon, now that it was happening.

"If it becomes an issue, I promise I'll tell you. But will you trust me when I say I need your help?"

Christi nodded, and sipped her tea, which was now lukewarm.

"I'll make another," Aunt Olivia said. "And then we'll get some lunch. Oh, look, there's Oscar coming!" Still carrying the kettle, Aunt Olivia went over to the little shuttered windows, pushed one open and called out of it.

"Oscar, I'm just putting the kettle on. Come and meet my niece!"

Aware that her eyes were probably red and blotchy from crying, Christi quickly blotted them with some kitchen roll. She didn't want to make a bad impression on her aunt's gardener, or whatever it was she had said Oscar did.

The man who entered the kitchen was not at all what she was expecting. He was young – her age, or thereabouts, she thought – with dark hair and black stubble across his face. He wore a black T-shirt that showed off impressive bicep muscles, and his skin was clearly tanned from working outside all the time. When he looked towards her, she saw his eyes were a rich brown, and his full lips pulled up into a smile.

"Hi," he said. "Oscar Reynolds. Nice to meet you." He held his hands up in the air. "I'd shake your hand but I'm covered in mud. I've finished digging that trench, Olivia – so just let me know what's next."

Christi found her tongue at last. "Christi King," she

said, with a little wave that she immediately cringed at. "Nice to meet you."

"Oscar is a godsend," Aunt Olivia said, as she busied herself with making more tea. "I don't know what I'd do without him."

"Oh, I think you'd be just fine," Oscar said. There was a slight West Country twang to his voice, and his eyes seemed to twinkle when he smiled.

"I most certainly would not. Don't go getting any ideas about abandoning me. I need your muscles here, thank you very much!"

Oscar laughed. Christi's eyes darted to said muscles. When she saw him watching her she blushed and turned back to her now-cold cup of tea.

"I've got a list, I'll get it for you. Christi is going to stay for the summer, and help me out, so you'll have plenty of time to get to know each other!"

Christi continued to look at her tea, so she couldn't do or say anything embarrassing.

"Oh, I know, why don't you take her into Salcombe tonight, Oscar, show her where the young people drink!"

Christi looked up quickly, feeling her cheeks burning red. "It's fine, Aunt Olivia, I'm sure Oscar has plans."

Aunt Olivia looked to Oscar, not seeming to see anything awkward about the situation. "Do you have plans, Oscar?"

He smiled and ran a hand through his cropped dark hair. "No plans," he said. He looked at Christi. "I can show you all the young, hip spots if you like," he said with a laugh. "Although I'm not that young anymore, and I don't know if I've ever been hip!"

Christi wasn't too impressed at being set up on her first night in town. But she didn't really feel she could say no, not without being rude to Aunt Olivia – and to Oscar. It had been quite some time since she'd been out for a drink with a man as handsome as him. Even if it was set up by her aunt, it wasn't an opportunity she thought she ought to turn down.

She had some time to settle into the floral bedroom at the back of the house, which she had stayed in when she had last visited. She had forgotten that the room had such a spectacular view of the ocean, and once she had unpacked her suitcases, she stood with her elbows leant against the wooden windowsill, looking out at the waves in the distance. They looked fairly calm at present, but then it had been a nice day. She wondered how it would look in a storm. But then, if the summer was everything she hoped, she would never find out. She would be back in London by the autumn, after all.

There was a soft knock at the door and she jumped, realising she had been daydreaming. She reached for the door and pulled it open to find her aunt standing on the other side.

"Just checking everything is okay," she said.

"Perfect, thank you. I'd forgotten how beautiful the view is!"

Aunt Olivia sighed. "The third bedroom – or the office, as it is now – looks out over the field, but mine and this one are lucky enough to face the sea. It was one of the reasons I just had to buy the place."

"And you like running a campsite?" Christi asked. She didn't want to sound rude, but it was quite an unusual profession, after all.

"I love meeting new people," she said. "And getting

to live near the coast, too. It's a win-win, really."

Privately, Christi wondered how it could possibly make enough money, but she didn't say that out loud.

"I feel bad, leaving you alone on my first night here," she said.

"Oh, don't be silly. I was the one that pushed you into it, anyway!"

Christi couldn't stop the smirk from playing on her lips. That was certainly true.

"You deserve to have a good time. And I'm afraid I'm rather set in my ways, and I'm in bed by nine at the latest."

Christi frowned. "But the other night, you messaged me back at some ridiculous hour of the morning!"

"Early to bed, early to rise," Aunt Olivia said with a tip of her head. "Although that was even earlier than I usually wake up. I don't always sleep that well – but I'll make sure to keep it down, if I'm up at an unsociable hour."

"Don't worry about me," Christi said. "It's your house."

"And yours, for however long you want," Aunt Olivia said with a beaming grin. "Now, Oscar said he'd pick you up at eight, so I'll make sure we've eaten before then.

Christi found herself feeling nervous as eight o'clock approached. The handsome gardener, or whatever his job title was, had made her go tongue-tied in Aunt Olivia's kitchen. Would she find it easier to talk to him over a drink?

The set-up by Aunt Olivia had seemed rather blatant, but at least Oscar had been in the room when it had happened. He would know that Christi had been as surprised by it as he had. That made it slightly less embarrassing.

CHAPTER NINE

She had taken a shower before dinner, and changed into a pair of black skinny jeans and a lightweight blue shirt that seemed suitable for the early summer weather. She presumed they were just going to some pub, but she wanted to make a bit of an effort.

At exactly eight o'clock, there was a tap on the front door, and Aunt Olivia hurried to answer it. Christi took the opportunity to check her appearance quickly in the mirror, making sure was nothing her teeth from the dinner that she had recently finished.

"Hi," she said, a little shyly, as Oscar entered the room.

He raised a hand in greeting. "Hi," he said. He was wearing dark jeans himself, and a pale shirt that was rolled up, showing his impressive arm muscles. Did he always have them on display? She supposed if she had muscles as impressive as his, she wouldn't want to hide them away either.

"Well, have a good time you two," Aunt Olivia said, practically herding them out of the door.

"Have you got a spare key, Aunt Olivia?" Christi asked. "In case you're in bed when I get back." After all, it was eight o'clock now. It wouldn't be long, if what her aunt said was true, until she was fast asleep.

"Ah, there'll be one somewhere, but I'll just leave

it open tonight, don't worry." Christi frowned. Things in the country were certainly different than she was used to in London.

"Okay..." she said, still feeling a little unsure about that idea.

Behind Aunt Olivia's tiny car, a dark green truck was parked. It was the sort of vehicle that would have been no use in the city, but considering his trade, she could see the benefits of it for Oscar. "I think I'm going to struggle around here, without being able to drive," she said, as much to herself as to Oscar.

She jumped at the sound of Oscar's deep voice, right by her ear, as he reached over her shoulder to open the door to the passenger side for her. "Yeah, it's not easy round here without a car. But I'm sure your aunt will be happy to drop you into Salcombe, or Kingsbridge. And let me know if you're stuck, I'm around here most days."

"Thank you," she said, pulling herself up into the truck and putting on the seat belt as he went round to the driver's side.

She didn't feel as sick in the truck as she had done in Aunt Olivia's little car, and she wondered if it was due to being so high up.

"Thanks for this," she said, filling the awkward silence. "I know Aunt Olivia kind of pushed you into it."

He glanced at her and smiled, before focusing his eyes back on the road. "It's no hardship. Don't worry."

Her stomach flipped a little at that comment. "Can you walk into Salcombe, from the campsite?" she asked to distract from her flushed cheeks.

"You can," he said. "Probably takes half an hour though, and that hill is a killer on the way back. Didn't know if you'd fancy it."

"That's very thoughtful of you," she said. Part of her bristled at him thinking she couldn't handle the walk... But it was nice of him to give up the chance to have a few drinks so she didn't have to. "I don't want to be the reason you can't have a good time, though," she said.

He grinned again. "I can have a good time on one drink, don't worry. Next time, maybe we'll walk."

He parked on a steep hill, yanking the handbrake on, and jumped out of the car as soon as he'd turned the lights off, opening the door for Christi. "It's quite a jump down," he said, offering his hand as he gave the words of explanation.

She wasn't used to such attention. She took his arm with a word of thanks and followed him along the main street of Salcombe. She'd been here before, but in the middle of the day, and the middle of summer. Now, the season had not quite begun, and it was dark. It wasn't quiet, but it wasn't the bustling road she remembered. They passed many shops with their doors locked but lights illuminating their displays of clothes or homeware. There were one or two pubs and restaurants, but he didn't stop at any of them, and she wondered where they were headed.

"Do you come into town often?" she asked.

"I live in a flat, just over there," he said, jerking his head towards a row of shops with flats above them. Christi thought they must have amazing views of the harbour, and wondered how he could afford to live in such a pricey town. But that, of course, would have been a very rude question to voice. "So I go to the pub or out for a meal fairly often."

She nodded, struggling to keep up with him as the road began to incline. His legs were far longer than hers, and she had to do two steps to keep up with one of his.

"Do you travel around much, with your work?" she asked.

He glanced back at her, and the moonlight caught his dark eyes. She nearly gasped at the jolt of awareness that thrummed through her body.

What was he doing, looking at women with eyes like that, making them weak at the knees? It didn't seem fair.

He seemed to notice that she was struggling to keep up and slowed his pace, although thankfully without mentioning it. "I've got a few properties I manage in Salcombe, then some in Malborough, some in Thurlestone. I love the view of Thurlestone Rock from those, so they're probably my favourites. I don't tend to go much further afield, unless the job pays particularly well!"

He laughed, and she laughed along with him, trying to remember the places he was mentioning. They'd driven through Malborough, on their way to Salcombe from the train station, she was sure. But Thurlestone... She'd have to ask Aunt Olivia where that was, and what was so special about this rock.

"You live in London, right?" he asked.

Did she? Currently she was homeless: staying with Aunt Olivia, but only temporarily. Where was her home? She supposed it was in London, although it was hard to imagine herself back in her waterlogged flat.

"Yeah," she said. "Near Islington."

"Bet that's pricey," he said, flashing a grin her way.

"Ridiculously so," she said with a roll of her eyes. "My flat's the size of a shoe box, but it's central, so I don't have to spend hours on the tube commuting to work.

Well..." Her voice trailed off as she suddenly remembered she didn't actually have a job anymore. "I didn't have to, anyway," she said, her voice dwindling as she finished the sentence.

"Did something happen?" he asked, finally stopping at the top of a set of steps. A sign told her the steps led to a pub, and she was relieved that their journey was at an end, and that he wasn't leading her somewhere dangerous in the dark. Perhaps he was right in thinking that she wouldn't have liked to walk down to the pub and back to the campsite. Everything seemed so dark out here, without the rows of streetlights she was used to.

"I was made redundant," she said, following him down the steps. The pub at the bottom glowed warmly in the dark night, and she was very much looking forward to a glass of wine. "Last week."

"Ah," he said, pushing the door open and holding it for her. "I'm sorry. That explains the sudden desire for a summer in Devon, then."

"Can't I just want to spend the summer with my aunt?" Christi said, a little irritated.

"You can," Oscar said. "But usually there's a reason for people to up sticks and move, even for a couple of months. Just makes more sense now, that's all."

He was right, and it annoyed her somewhat that he could read her so well. But then he asked what she wanted, and bought her a glass of wine, and soon they were sat at a wooden table, just about able to make out waves in the distance, under the light of a nearly-full moon.

"Was it a good decision, then, do you think?" he asked, taking a swig from a bottle of beer.

"I've not been here twenty-four hours yet," Christi

said with a laugh. "Give me a chance to make my mind up."

"Your aunt is great, though. You'll have a good summer, I'm sure."

Christi nodded, wondering if she should voice her concerns. She didn't want any of it getting back to Aunt Olivia, and it upsetting or offending her, but there was no one else she could talk to about it, either. "To be honest," she said, taking a sip of her wine and savouring it. "I'm not really sure why I'm here. Aunt Olivia said she needed help on the campsite, that there were loads of bookings… But it doesn't look any different to me than when she bought it seven years ago."

Oscar tapped his fingers on the side of the bottle of beer. "I…" He paused and glanced at her, his eyes boring into hers. "I wouldn't want to say anything out of turn."

Christi shook her head. "I love my aunt. I'm not trying to bad mouth her, or spread gossip, or anything like that."

"I don't think the campsite makes very much," he said with a shrug. "And I don't think she has much to put back into it."

Christi bit her lip. "That's what I feared… But then I don't understand why she's told me she needs my help."

"Maybe she wants to help you out?" Oscar asked, taking a swig from the brown glass bottle.

"I don't want her to help me at her cost, though. I thought she actually needed someone to work on the campsite."

"I think she's lonely," Oscar said. "And the physical aspect of running the campsite is a lot for her."

"Isn't that what you're for? With your impressive muscles?" Christi felt her face flaming red. She couldn't believe she'd said that out loud. "I mean–"

He laughed, an easy carefree sound that rang out through the little pub. "Well, I'm glad someone is noticing all those hours at the gym," he said. "I do the digging and the mowing and the planting, yeah," he said. "But that's not every day, and not all year round. When people are here they ask for help with setting up, and things break down, and money has to be collected – it's a lot of work, even when the place isn't overrun with guests."

"I'm happy to help," Christi said, her cheeks still flaming, feeling like she wasn't coming across very well in this conversation. "And I would have come down just to see her. But I don't want her feeling like she *has* to give me a job, if there isn't one. That's all."

"Well, if you want my opinion," Oscar said, picking at the beer bottle label absentmindedly, "I'd let your aunt make that decision. Have a great summer, enjoy Salcombe, spend some time with your aunt, save on rent – and trust that she'll tell you if she can't afford you."

It was basically what Aunt Olivia herself had said, but she bristled slightly at hearing it from Oscar. She *would* have happily come down to stay if her aunt was lonely – although a voice in the back of her mind said that she hadn't been down in many years.

But she had been busy. Aunt Olivia understood that. And as she herself had said, she'd not been up to London, either.

This was a great opportunity to spend time with the only member of her family that she felt she could be herself around.

CHAPTER TEN

Having forgotten to close the curtains the night before, she woke up feeling the sun on her face and stretched out, forgetting for a moment where she was. When she opened her eyes and realised she couldn't see her oven from her bed, the memory of the campsite came flooding back and she smiled to herself.

The sun was shining and she was going to have a good day.

Aunt Olivia was nowhere to be found when she padded into the kitchen, so she rifled through the cupboard above the kettle to find the coffee and made herself a strong one. She hadn't been out particularly late, but she had drunk three glasses of wine. The busy day had caught up with her as soon as she'd said goodnight to Oscar, locked the front door (surely Aunt Olivia didn't sleep with the door unlocked) and slipped into the bed that was hers for the next few weeks. She'd drifted into a deep sleep almost immediately, and without an alarm to wake her, had slept until nearly nine.

She felt guilty, but they hadn't actually said when she would start work. She hoped Aunt Olivia wouldn't mind, whenever she reappeared. Glancing outside, she saw that her little car was still on the drive. So presumably she was out on the campsite.

Once she'd thrown on some jeans and a T-shirt, she

took her coffee out for a walk to find her aunt. She wanted to see the place properly, anyway – and find out what exactly her aunt wanted her to do here for the summer.

It was sad to see how few tents were pitched, although, as both Oscar and Aunt Olivia had pointed out, the season hadn't started yet. Once the kids broke up for their summer holidays, she hoped there would be an influx of campers.

At the top of the field, she stopped and looked around. The view of the sea, sparkling in the distance, was spectacular. She wasn't a big fan of camping herself – if she could afford a holiday, she really wanted a hotel – but she could definitely see the appeal of this location. A small copse of trees at the top of the hill provided some shade from the sun, and she stood there for a moment looking out over Salcombe. It was beautiful. If only the amenities weren't so tired... And there were more of them.

Perhaps she could help her aunt, even if the campsite was quiet. Maybe she could help draw in some new campers...

She shielded her eyes from the sunshine, which was growing in warmth by the minute, and scanned the field for her aunt. Her eyes alighted on a figure in the far corner of the field. She was wearing a straw hat, but it was the dress that made her sure it was her aunt, despite the distance. Today's was covered in tulips, and it was very definitely the sort of dress Aunt Olivia would choose.

Her aunt was talking to someone by a tent, so Christi leant against a fence post and drank her coffee, enjoying the view. The field was mowed perfectly short, and she remembered Oscar saying that was one of his duties. She blushed, remembering her compliment of his muscles, and then tried to shrug it off. If they were both going to be working here all summer, she couldn't become tongue-tied around him, or be flustered by his good looks. He was a handsome man, yes – but that didn't mean she had to let his looks affect her.

"Morning!" Aunt Olivia called, making her way across the field, and Christi shook away the thoughts of Oscar and smiled at her aunt.

"Sorry, I didn't mean to sleep in so late."

Aunt Olivia waved away her concerns. "Don't worry about it. Did you have a nice time, with Oscar?"

There was a suggestive tone to her voice that Christi chose to ignore.

"Lovely, thank you," she said. "Now, I need to know what you want me to do around here. What my job actually is. I don't want to be just getting under your feet."

They walked back towards the house together, with Aunt Olivia mentioning needing a cup of tea.

"You should take today to get settled in," Aunt Olivia said. "Ring your parents, tell them you're here…"

Christi sighed. She knew she would have to ring them, but it was not an appealing thought.

"Okay. But after that? What were you doing, just now?"

"I was just collecting money from one of the campers."

"They still pay in cash?" Christi asked, surprised. She never had cash on her these days.

"Oh yes. Or bank transfer. I haven't managed to get a card machine sorted, although I do get asked a lot…"

"Well, that's something I could definitely help with," Christi said. "If you wanted me to."

Aunt Olivia grinned and pushed open the front

door. "Of course. And you could take a look at the website, too, if you fancied it. One of the local girls set it up for me, years ago, but I've not got a clue what I'm doing with it."

"I can do that. And are you online anywhere else? Social media?"

Aunt Olivia screwed up her face. "I don't really like all of that stuff."

"I get that," Christi said, filling up the kettle and putting it on the range. "But it can be really helpful in getting your name out there. I can do that too..." She was beginning to feel more confident about her place here. The campsite might not be busy, but perhaps she could make it busier. She knew advertising, after all. And the internet was no mystery to her.

"You can have free rein, dear. Whatever you think."

"But you'll have to tell me what else you want me to do. Collecting money? Cleaning?"

"Cleaning the shower block would be helpful, if you don't mind..."

Christi didn't relish the thought of cleaning the showers and toilets, but she wasn't going to say that. "I'm here to work, Aunt Olivia. I'll do whatever needs doing. I can clean them today, if you like..."

"Tomorrow's fine, dear. Take today to settle in. And we should discuss pay and time off and–"

"I trust you're not going to work me into the ground," Christi said as the kettle began to whistle. "And you're giving me food and board, too." She did not want her aunt to have no income from the summer because she had offered her a place to stay, even if she had been a little economical with the truth when it came to the state of the campsite.

Later that day, while Aunt Olivia made them lunch,

Christi pulled out her laptop and looked at the campsite's website. She had never seen it before and it made her cringe. It looked like it belonged in the nineties, with about five different fonts, a dark blue background and flashing stars across the page. She had no idea what the stars were meant to be for, and it was hard to read. The price list looked ridiculously cheap, and she wondered if it had ever been updated since it was set up.

Well, this was something she could definitely help with.

"Did you ring your parents yet?" Aunt Olivia asked, setting a plate with a sandwich, crisps and salad in front of Christi.

Christi sighed as the thoughts of the new website she could design were chased from her head.

"No. I will do…"

"After lunch?" Aunt Olivia said. It was phrased as a question, but Christi knew she had to do it. Otherwise they would call, and she would have to lie, or announce it out of the blue, like she'd been caught doing something wrong. Or, even worse, they'd end up calling her work, and find out that she'd lost her job.

"I guess so."

She disappeared into her room to make the call, although Aunt Olivia had gone outside again. She seemed to spend much of her time outside, although Christi wasn't entirely sure what she was doing. She didn't want her aunt – or anyone else – coming in during this conversation, which was sure to be awkward.

Christi tried her dad first, because he tended to keep conversations shorter, and ask fewer questions, but there was no response. Part of her considered putting off the task to another day, but deep down she knew it had to be done.

So, with a deep breath, she scrolled to her mum's number and hit dial.

If she didn't answer, would that be a reprieve? Or would it be worse, left hanging over her?

Just as she was about to give up and cancel the call, her mother's voice came down the line.

CHAPTER ELEVEN

"Good afternoon, Emma King speaking."

Always the same, even though she surely knew it was her daughter. "Hi, Mum," Christi said.

"Hello, Christi darling. How are you? I'm afraid I've got a client meeting in about ten minutes…"

"That's okay," Christi said, somewhat relieved that it could not be a long call. "I only called quickly, to let you know…" She bit her bottom lip. "I just wanted you to know that I'm at Aunt Olivia's, for the summer."

There was silence on the other end of the line, and Christi pulled her phone away from her ear to check they had not been disconnected.

"I thought we agreed that wasn't a sensible option," her mother finally said, her voice steely. "If my sister has been guilt-tripping you–"

"Aunt Olivia hasn't persuaded me into this, Mum," Christi said, rolling her eyes and trying not to sound too irritated. "I wanted a break. She offered me somewhere to go. That's all. I just didn't want you and Dad not to know where I was."

"What about your job, Christi? And your flat?"

"It'll be there when I get back," she said. Her mother didn't need to know she was only referring to the flat. And even that was only a maybe.

"I don't understand how you can mess with your

career like this, Christi. For a few weeks in Devon. Doing what, anyway?"

"I'll work, help out Aunt Olivia... It's beautiful here," she said, trying to inject some positivity into this miserable conversation.

"I know it's beautiful, Christi. But beauty isn't going to pay the rent, or get you a promotion, is it. Look, I don't want to sound–"

Christi cut her mother off. She couldn't hear any more of it. And she definitely didn't want to hear criticism of Aunt Olivia, when she had offered Christi a way out.

Not that her mother knew that.

"Mum. It's fine. I know what I'm doing, I promise. You get to your meeting – we'll speak soon."

And then she hung up the phone and lay back on her bed, groaning loudly.

There was a knock on the door and Christi called for the person – presuming it was her aunt – to enter, without sitting up.

"Oh. Sorry. I was just looking for Olivia–"

The distinctly male voice made her sit bolt upright. Oscar was standing in her doorway, shirtsleeves rolled up as always, and she was very pleased that she had only been in this room one night, and it was not a mess.

"Hi," she said. "Sorry, I thought you were Aunt Olivia."

"No worries. Everything okay?" he asked.

She wondered if he'd heard her phone call, or her groan of frustration when she had hung up on her mother.

"Just my parents, being judgmental," she said. "Nothing new. I think Aunt Olivia's out in the field somewhere, but I don't know where..."

Oscar frowned. "I was just out there and didn't see her. I'll look again. The picnic bench has rotted through. We're going to need to replace it before the season starts or it'll be a hazard."

Christi nodded. "I'll come and help you find her," she said, following him from the room. "And while we walk – have you got any ideas of how to improve this place, without spending a fortune? I want to help Aunt Olivia all I can, but I don't really know anything about camping..."

"Did you speak to your parents?" Aunt Olivia asked the next day at breakfast. Although they'd spent the evening together, the topic hadn't come up, and Christi had been happy enough to avoid it.

"Yeah," Christi said, buttering her toast with more force than was probably necessary.

"All okay?"

Christi liked that Aunt Olivia never forced her to give more information than she was willing. It was a nice change of pace.

"Not really. Mum's not impressed that I'm down here, thinks I'm throwing my life away... Obviously I didn't tell her about the mess I'm in at home."

"She'll just think I'm leading you astray," Aunt Olivia said with a cackle.

"Well..." Christi said, not wanting to upset her aunt by admitting she was right.

"Oh, don't worry about me dear. I've got a thick skin. I won't tell them why you left London, even if they want to blame me for luring you down here."

"You're the only person in this family I can talk to, Aunt Olivia," Christi said, reaching over and squeezing her aunt's hand. Her eyes felt damp and she blinked. "Thank you. For letting me come here."

Aunt Olivia squeezed her hand back. "I'm always here for you, Christi. I'm glad you came."

Feeling a little overwhelmed by her own emotions, Christi focused on her toast for several minutes.

"I've got to go into Kingsbridge today, to get some things from the supermarket," Aunt Olivia said. "If you want to come."

"Thanks," Christi said. "I want to clean the shower block this morning, and then start looking at the website, too – but there's a couple of things I could do with."

With three weeks until the school holidays, and the bookings for the campsite reaching nowhere near capacity, Christi was keen to get the word out online that the campsite was open and beautiful. She took advantage of the beautiful weather over the next few days to take photos – not including the dilapidated shower block – making sure to show off the gorgeous view that the campsite boasted. She spent a whole day, minus the hour she spent cleaning, redesigning the website. It took nearly another whole day to get the details of the web host sorted so that the nineties monstrosity was no longer linked to the campsite's URL. Then it was time to create social media accounts, and make sure that if people were looking for a Devon campsite, they actually found Sunset Shore Campsite.

It felt good to use her advertising skills, and she was excited to show her aunt the campsite's new online presence. If more people booked to camp, then perhaps they could put some money back into the campsite... And she had a list of ideas of things that could be improved, thanks to Oscar, if they had the funds to do it.

"Wow," Aunt Olivia said as they sat out in the garden and had a cup of tea one evening. So far, the early summer had proven beautiful, and Christi only hoped the fine weather continued once the kids had broken up from school. If the summer was a washout, she couldn't imagine her plans would be very helpful to her aunt. That was the problem with holidaying in England: the weather was just so unpredictable.

"I can hardly recognise it! And the website, it looks so modern."

Christi smiled. She wasn't a designer, by any means, but she was pleased with what she had created. "You like it?"

"I do. You're very clever. And those photos are beautiful. I just… Wouldn't want people expecting more than we've got."

"I haven't lied about anything," Christi reassured her. "Just maybe…been a bit economical with the angles. It's nothing estate agents don't do all the time."

Aunt Olivia nodded. "Well, I trust you dear. And I'm very impressed with what you've done in such a short amount of time. And that shower block is gleaming!"

Christi felt a warm glow at the praise, although beneath the surface she felt a little concerned. It was nice that Aunt Olivia trusted her – but what if this didn't work? What if people did feel duped by the new photos and the fancy website? Then it would all be on her.

Their days together fell into a comfortable routine. Christi woke up after Aunt Olivia, but they had breakfast together before Christi went out to clean, and sometimes to collect money from the campers. She ordered a card machine, knowing that it made sense for the campsite to have one, and was just waiting for it to turn up.

They would sit and have lunch together, too. And most days when Oscar was on site, doing whatever work needed to be done, Aunt Olivia tended to ask him to join them. And Christi did enjoy his company. He was good-looking, of course, but he was also funny, and told interesting stories, and added a different dynamic to their day.

But she couldn't help but find him distracting. He made her mind a little scrambled, and she often felt like a bit of a fool. She couldn't even explain it. She had been around handsome men before, so why was he so different? And it wasn't like there was anything between them. They'd been out for that drink, but that had been organised by Aunt Olivia. He had certainly not suggested that they go out again. And she had no plans to ask him. He was a work colleague – nothing more. So there was no reason for her mind to scramble in his presence.

And then there were the looks that Aunt Olivia gave her. When she thought she wasn't looking. Did she think she was being subtle? Christi only hoped that Oscar wouldn't pick up on her embarrassing behaviour. Or if he did, that he realised it was all Aunt Olivia, and nothing to do with Christi.

With just over a week until the beginning of the school holidays, bookings had increased a fair amount, and Christi was cautiously optimistic about her plan.

But then a set of the new campers arrived... And proved Aunt Olivia right.

Oh, they were polite about it. But Christi noticed their faces fall when they saw the basic campsite, and when she went to their tent to take their money (the card machine having been inexplicably delayed) the father of the group raised his concerns. "There's not much here, is there."

"Authentic, rustic, rural camping," Christi said with a forced smile. It was what she'd put on the website, after all.

"The view is spectacular," he said. "But we'd hoped there would be a bit more to do, on the campsite. And the facilities…"

He glanced at the sad-looking shower block, and Christi felt an embarrassed blush spreading across her face.

"The weather is set to be lovely," she said, not really addressing his concerns. "And we've got brochures for ferry trips, and information on all the best local beaches. There really is so much to do around here."

The man nodded, and smiled, and although he wasn't angry at her, she thought she might have felt better if he had been. She had seen the disappointment on his face at the campsite. And although she knew she hadn't lied, she had done everything she could to sell the campsite.

And she had succeeded. But she wasn't confident in repeat customers.

She had to do something. If the campsite got a bad reputation, it would be on her – and that was certainly a poor way to repay her aunt's kindness.

She stumbled across Oscar, carrying a picnic bench by himself from the back of his truck. He grunted with the effort of it, his muscles straining, and Christi stayed out of the way. She was fairly sure that offering to help would only make the job harder.

When he had put it down on the grass that had

been vacated by the previous rotting one, she decided to see if he had any ideas of how they could kick-start things.

"When we talked the other day," she said. "You had lots of ideas, about the campsite."

Oscar nodded, stretching out his arms after lifting the heavy bench.

"I think I need to try to implement some, soon."

"Oh?" Oscar said, raising an eyebrow.

"I've got more people booked in... But I think they're expecting...more."

"A lot of the newer campsites have a lot more in the way of amenities," Oscar said. "But I didn't think your aunt had the money to sink into it..."

"I don't think she has," Christi said, with a sigh. "So I want to see what I can do at low-to-no cost."

"Behind your aunt's back?" Oscar said, looking concerned.

"No. Well, she's said I can do what I need to. I wasn't going to share any specifics with her... Until it works. Or we've got a plan. Or something."

Somehow this had morphed from 'I' to 'we', and she hoped that Oscar was willing to help her. She knew what she was doing with the online side of things, but when it came to physical improvements, she was pretty clueless.

"Okay..." he said slowly, glancing around the large field. "Well, there's only one thing here we can improve, really, isn't there."

They both looked to the shower block. It was made of concrete, but there were cracks and chips and weathered marks, and it did not look appealing in the slightest.

But how could they improve it?

"I've not got much money," she said. "I'd put it in, if I did."

"I doubt your aunt would want you putting your own money in, anyway," he said. "Let me have a think what we can do, okay?"

"Thanks, Oscar," Christi said with a shy smile. "I do really appreciate your help. My aunt's lucky to have you around."

Oscar shrugged and ran a hand through his dark hair, seemingly embarrassed by the compliment. "Your aunt's always been very good to me. I'm happy to help her out, if I can. And you."

Their eyes met and Christi felt a prickle of awareness through her body. She swallowed, and glanced away just as quickly.

"I'll see if I can think of anything else, too. Maybe something we could add... Oh, it would be helpful if I actually knew anything about camping!"

Oscar laughed and went on with his day, and Christi brushed off the odd feeling and disappeared inside to do some research.

CHAPTER TWELVE

"I'm insisting you take the day off," Aunt Olivia said. "You've worked every day since you got here, bookings are up-"

Customer satisfaction is not, though, Christi thought to herself. She didn't mention her concerns to her aunt, hoping that she could fix the issue before anyone raised it with her.

"I'm here to work, Aunt Olivia," Christi said with a roll of her eyes over their morning tea.

"Not every minute of every day, you're not. You've done so much already."

"You're happy with me doing whatever I think will get more customers in, though?" she asked, wanting to ensure that if she did makeover the shower block, or any of the other ideas she had got from a night of internet searching, her aunt wouldn't be upset.

"Of course. You've got a real eye for these things. But still, I want you to have a day off."

"I don't even know what I'd do," Christi said with a half smile.

"You're in Devon, the weather is lovely. What would you like to do?"

Christi thought for a moment. "Well, go to the beach, I suppose."

"Perfect. I'll pack you a lunch."

"It's a shame you can't come with me," Christi said. It felt a bit pathetic to go to the beach alone, and it wasn't as though she had any friends here.

"I can't leave the place unattended dear, I'm afraid. If we can get someone to watch it next week, I will."

Christi nodded, feeling a bit like a child being placated.

"You've got a swimming costume?" her aunt asked.

"I've not worn it in forever... But yes, I've got a bikini."

"Excellent. I'll get you a towel – and you should take a book down. Enjoy the sunshine for a few hours."

"Can I walk to the beach?" Christi asked, feeling a bit silly. She hadn't left the campsite, except for the drink with Oscar, and one trip to the supermarket, in the two weeks since she had arrived.

"You could, but I can drop you down I'm sure. When Oscar comes by, I'll get him to hang around for ten minutes while I take you. He won't mind. He's a good lad. Handsome, too."

And then she winked at Christi.

"Aunt Olivia!" Christi exclaimed. "You're very transparent, you know, and you need to stop! Yes, he's handsome, but that doesn't mean something will happen between us."

There was a brief knock before the front door swung open, and Oscar raised his hand in greeting.

"Morning," he said, and Christi's cheeks flushed bright red.

Had he heard her call him handsome?

"Good morning, Oscar. Do you want a coffee, before you get started?"

"No, thanks," Oscar said. "I've got to get over to

Thurlestone before eleven, so I'm only stopping by to sort that fence post, and I'll be off. Just wanted to see if you needed anything else doing, since I won't be around for the rest of the day."

"Oh!" Aunt Olivia said, her eyes sparkling as she looked at Christi. "Well. I was going to ask if you could hold the fort for ten minutes, while I drop Christi down at the beach."

"Course I can," Oscar said.

"But if you're going to Thurlestone – perhaps you could drop her down at the beach there? I think she'd love it."

"Oh, I don't want to be a bother, Oscar has a busy work day," Christi insisted, her cheeks feeling even hotter. Hadn't she just told her aunt to be less obvious? "Besides, how would I get back? It's fine, I don't need to go to Thurlestone, I–"

"I'm happy to take you down," Oscar said. "And in all honesty, I was planning on a dip in the sea after work, so I could bring you back. If you were happy to stay down there until four-ish."

Christi swallowed. She really didn't want to be a burden. And the thought of him in only swimming trunks did things to her mind that it really shouldn't.

"Perfect," Aunt Olivia said, clapping her hands together. "Isn't it lovely when everything works out."

"I'm glad your aunt suggested this," Oscar said as they drove out of Salcombe in his green truck, the sun high in the sky, Christi's bag shoved down by her feet.

Her heart skipped a beat. Why was he appreciative of her aunt's obvious matchmaking?

"I had some ideas," he said. "About the shower block."

Christi felt embarrassed, even though he had no idea of the thoughts in her head. She was stupid for letting his handsome face and impressive body make her mind turn to mush.

"Oh? Something cheap, I hope," she said with a laugh.

"Yeah. The inside is actually pretty decent. It's the outside that's awful. I've got a mate who's getting rid of a shed, and I was thinking we could just…rehouse it. Not get rid of anything, but add another layer."

Christi nodded thoughtfully, thinking over his proposal. "That would be doable, would it? I mean, I don't have a clue how anything like that works…"

He laughed. "I could put it up, yeah. And it would be safe."

"I can't really pay you any more than Aunt Olivia does…"

"I'm not doing it for money," he said. "I'm happy to offer my time, as much use as it is."

"Oh, it's a lot of use," Christi said. "And I wonder if any of the locals are good at painting, and might be willing to do a mural or something on it. That could make a big difference, making it a feature, rather than something we're embarrassed of."

Oscar turned to her and frowned, and then looked back at the road. It was far twistier than the road from Salcombe to Kingsbridge, and Christi felt her stomach rolling a little every time they went round a corner.

"Ignoring the obvious, you mean?"

"Who's the obvious?"

"Your aunt."

"She paints?"

"You didn't know?"

Christi shook her head. "She's never mentioned it."

"Well, she'd be the one to ask, if you're wanting a mural."

"This sounds like it could work," Christi said, feeling excited. "And I was also thinking – although I need your advice on this, I'm afraid – that maybe we could have some sort of fire pit? And provide marshmallows for toasting? It would be cheap, I think, but kids would love it."

Oscar grinned. "I love a toasted marshmallow."

"Not just kids then," she said with a giggle. "Do you think it could work?"

"Yeah, I do. We'd have to pick the site carefully, make sure it's safe... I can help with that, though."

"Thanks, Oscar. I don't think the campsite could cope without you!"

He dropped her off by a path that wound past a golf course and down to the beach. "You'll be okay till four?"

She nodded. "I'm a big girl, I can look after myself, I promise!"

"Here's my number," he said, handing her a business card. "In case you need it... Although I don't think you'll get any signal down here."

She took it, and as their fingers brushed that odd feeling was back again. "Thanks for the lift," she said, ignoring it. "Hope your job goes well."

"Thanks," he said. "It's not far away, just on the outskirts of the village. They want a pond digging so–" He flexed one arm. "My impressive muscles must come to the rescue."

Christi laughed, and blushed, and grabbed her bag

from the truck. "Thanks for the lift," she said. "I'll see you later."

CHAPTER THIRTEEN

The beach was beautiful. The water sparkled under the sunlight, and when she removed her shoes, the sand crunched between her toes. She took a deep breath of the salty air and smiled, feeling content.

It was a small beach, with a pile of rocks at one end and the glittering sea stretching out into the distance. There were not many people on it, and she was rather surprised by that, considering the beautiful weather. When the weather was like this back in London, the parks were packed. But then, it was the middle of the workday. She supposed people were still at work, children still at school, and of course, the holidaymakers had not yet arrived.

In the middle of the sea, a clear beacon for anyone looking for it, was the rock that she presumed was the Thurlestone rock that Oscar had referred to. A tall, rounded monolith, with a hole through the middle. She presumed it had formed naturally, for she could see no reason why it would be man-made. How tempting it looked to swim out and through the hole, but it was rather a long way in the distance, and she was not the strongest swimmer. In fact, she had rarely swum in an open body of water like this before.

There were a couple of families with young children dotted along the beach, as well as the odd dog walker. A man in a wetsuit was on a surfboard, paddling out into the sea. At the water's edge, some young children jumped in the waves, and one watched his father skim a stone. For a few moments she walked along the golden sands, her shoes in one hand, her bag in the other. It was nice just to feel the sand beneath her toes, to look out into all this space and appreciate where she was. The sun was warm, pleasantly so, and when she reached the far side of the beach, she laid out her towel and sat beside the rocks.

She was quite keen to swim now that she was here – but she wanted to be thoroughly warmed up. As enticing as the ocean looked, she was fairly sure it was going to be freezing. After all, wasn't that what everyone said about the sea in England?

She lay back, using her jumper as a makeshift pillow, and closed her eyes. She could hear the children playing, seagulls squawking in the distance, and the waves gently lapping against the shore. She took a deep breath, held it, and then let it out. Everything was going to be all right. She would fix the issues she had caused with the website and the high expectations. Between them, she and Oscar would build the new exterior for the shower block, and she would ask Aunt Olivia to paint a mural. She felt terribly guilty that she had no idea about Aunt Olivia's painting talent, but she was sure her aunt had never mentioned it. Neither had her mother. She supposed they saw painting as a frivolous pastime.

So, she would make everything right with the site. And she had the whole, glorious summer stretched out ahead of her. She loved waking up every morning and hearing the peace and quiet outside the windows, knowing that her aunt would be around, the kettle would soon be whistling, and that she had a list of tasks to accomplish.

And after the summer? Would everything be all right then? She couldn't really think about it. There was nothing she could do, really. The flat situation... Well, she supposed that would work itself out. And at some point, she needed to start applying for jobs for the autumn. But even thinking about it made her heart race, and she just wanted to not worry for just a short period, to not feel stressed and anxious.

The day passed far more quickly than she had anticipated. She had changed into her bikini behind the privacy of the rocks, but every time she considered dipping in the sea, she wondered whether it was totally sensible. The tide didn't look very rough... But what if it washed her away? This was too small a beach for a lifeguard, and she wasn't sure that the scattered people on it would pay any attention to her if she were pulled under by a rogue wave. Wasn't there something said about never swimming alone?

And so she sat and ate the picnic that Aunt Olivia had packed for her and read her book, digging her toes into the wet sand. Before she knew it, there was a crunching of footsteps behind her, and when she turned and shielded her eyes, Oscar was towering above her.

"Is it that time already?" she said, her heart jumping. "I totally lost track..."

"I finished a bit early," he said, shielding his eyes while looking out to sea. "Have you had a nice day?"

"Lovely, thank you. Was your job okay?"

"Another customer satisfied with my impressive muscles," he said with a wink.

Once again, Christi's face flushed a deep red, and she decided to tease him back to make things a little more even. "You sound like you're selling your body, saying things like that."

He gave a short, sharp laugh. "Well, I suppose I am, in a way. Not in the way you're suggesting, though."

"Are you hungry?" Christi asked, holding out the lunchbox that Aunt Olivia had packed for her. "Aunt Olivia packed me more sandwiches than I could finish in a week."

"Starving, actually," Oscar said with a smile, helping himself to one of the sandwiches that was left. He demolished it in one go before asking, "You had a swim?"

Christi checked ahead. "Not yet," she said. "I was going to... But I wasn't sure how sensible it was to swim alone..."

"I mean, you can swim, right?"

"Of course I can!" Christi said, a little indignantly. "But I'm much more used to a pool than the sea."

"There's nothing quite like swimming in the sea," Oscar said, and before she knew what he was doing, he had pulled his T-shirt off over his head, revealing that his torso was indeed made up of impressive muscles.

Her mouth went dry, and she averted her eyes, knowing she was blushing. She was rather glad she had put her T-shirt and shorts back over her swimsuit – she would have felt entirely naked in his presence.

"Well then," he said, standing up and unbuttoning his shorts. Christi didn't know where to look. "You'll be perfectly fine. Besides, I'm going in – and I'm a strong swimmer, I promise you."

She was rather relieved when he dropped the denim shorts and revealed a pair of swimming trunks beneath them. She wondered when he put them on. This morning, before they'd even left? Or maybe in his car, before coming down to the beach.

She looked up at him, his bronzed, muscular body making it hard for her to think.

"Are you coming then?" he asked, offering her his hand to help her up from the towel. She forced her mouth closed and tried to get her mind back on the present. What was she doing? She wasn't some hormone-filled teenager. "Yeah. Yeah, that sounds great."

She gripped his hand and it was warm and strong as it pulled her up from the towel. A little too strong, perhaps: she stumbled forward, nearly landing on her face, ending up with her hands pressed against his torso, her nose inches from his skin.

She jumped back as though he had burned her. "Sorry, I–"

She would have been quite happy if a hole had opened up and swallowed her up right there.

But he only laughed. "It's fine," he said. "Are you swimming in your clothes?"

Christi shook her head, barely able to meet his eye. She knew her cheeks were bright red, but there was nothing she could do about it. Shyly, she pulled her T-shirt over her head, and her shorts quickly followed. It was not the most revealing bikini in the world, but it certainly showed a lot more of her skin than her clothes did, and she felt exposed. His eyes wandered her body for just a second before he jogged off in the direction of the sea. She felt warm, and not just from the sun. He made her feel things that she hadn't felt in quite some time. Things she shouldn't be feeling for the gardener at her aunt's campsite.

She followed him, feeling the warm sun on her newly exposed skin. She had dipped her toes in the water in the hours she had spent on the beach, and felt how cold it was, but when she followed him in and let the water pool around her calf muscles, she gasped.

He ploughed on, and she watched as he flexed his muscled arms and dived straight into the water. It made her shiver just to see him beneath the icy waves. When he resurfaced, laughing, she took a step forwards and tried to be as brave.

"It's freezing!" she said as he shook droplets of water from his dark hair.

"It's not so bad once you've got in," he said. "Refreshing, even." A devilish glint passed across his eyes. "Want me to help you?"

He lifted his hand as though to splash water at her and she instinctively closed her eyes and held up her hands to protect herself.

"No, thank you!" she said in a high-pitched voice.

"Well, don't take too long about it," he said. "It's worse the longer you wait!"

And with that he began to swim a very impressive front crawl across the length of the beach, and Christi just watched, feeling a fizzing in her body that she thought was probably quite dangerous.

He was a strong swimmer, and she wondered how often he swam in these waters. Soon he would surely turn and retrace his path, and she thought she ought to have dipped under the water by then. She counted to three and strode further into the water, pausing for a moment before giving herself another count to three to acclimatise. And then, with a deep breath, she plunged her body under the water, until it reached her neck.

She gasped. The cold took her breath away, and she was ready to call Oscar a liar and get out, when it started to get easier to breathe again. She moved her arms beneath the water. It wasn't warm, but it wasn't as shocking any more.

Carefully, she swam a gentle breaststroke parallel to the beach, and was feeling quite proud of herself when Oscar reappeared, all lean arms and strong, powerful legs.

He grinned at her. "Better?"

"Yes," she said, grudgingly. "I suppose so. But I'm not staying in for long!"

"Fair enough," he said with a laugh. "I'm going to do a few lengths of the beach while we're here, if you don't mind."

And that was how Christi found herself sitting on the warm sand, drying off from her swim, and watching Oscar cutting back and forth through the water.

She needed him to help her with her plans for the campsite, and he was very fun to be around. But she thought, before the end of the summer, that the flipping he caused in the pit of her stomach and the fuzziness in her brain might become a bit of a problem.

CHAPTER FOURTEEN

"Why didn't I know that you paint?" Christi asked her Aunt over breakfast, a few days after her beach trip with Oscar.

Aunt Olivia shrugged. "I don't know. I presumed you did. I've always done it – since I was a little kid." She poured another cup of tea from the floral teapot that sat in the centre of the kitchen table. "What makes you ask about it now?"

Christi paused, unsure how much to tell her aunt at this point. The plan was in motion, but she wondered if it should be complete before she revealed all.

"Oscar mentioned it," she said, buying some time. "When we were down at the beach."

Aunt Olivia frowned. "How on earth did that come up?"

"Well… I've got some ideas, for physical improvements around the place. And Oscar is helping me." She rushed to get the words out, realising she felt rather nervous about telling her aunt. What if she was offended? Or told Christi to stop?

"That's very kind of you both, but you know I haven't got the money right now – to pay Oscar any extra, or for renovations."

Christi shook her head. "No, you don't need to–"

"And I will not hear of you paying for it, do you hear me? The last thing you need is to be ploughing money into some old woman's business."

Christi laughed, and shook her head once more. "No – I mean, I would, but I don't really have much to spare myself. Not if I want to be able to pay rent come September. No, I – we – have had some ideas that don't cost anything, save Oscar volunteering to do the heavy lifting."

Was she blushing at the thought of Oscar's rippling muscles as he carried the heavy equipment? She hoped her cheeks only felt warm and that the redness was not visible. How ridiculous she was being.

"Oh," Aunt Olivia said, not commenting on Christi's red cheeks, if indeed they were visibly red. "Well, I suppose that's okay then. As long as you're not working too hard – either of you."

Christi rolled her eyes. "We're here to work, Aunt Olivia," she said, pouring herself a second cup of tea. She had never owned a teapot, but she did rather like drinking tea made in one. It tasted better somehow, although she knew that made no logical sense.

"But I still don't understand how the subject of me painting came up."

"Well..." Christi said, dragging the word out into multiple syllables. "I don't want to spoil the surprise. But as part of our plan, we might need a mural painting – and Oscar thought you were the obvious choice."

Aunt Olivia beamed. "What a wonderful idea. Silly really, that I've never thought to do it. Where will it be? Oh, I know, don't want to ruin the surprise." She rubbed her hands together excitedly. "This summer is going to be wonderful, I just know it."

Christi certainly hoped so. If this all went wrong... Well, all she was likely to gain was a handful of negative reviews for her aunt's campsite.

On the Sunday before the summer holidays began, Aunt Olivia asked Christi if she would be happy to mind the campsite for the day, while she went to Plymouth, the nearest city, to buy a new laptop. Christi had no idea why her aunt had a sudden desire to have a modern PC, but the timing was perfect. She and Oscar had planned to work on their renovation that day –and although Christi had assumed Aunt Olivia would see what they were doing, it was rather more exciting for her to be out and come back to the surprise.

"Thanks for giving up your day off," Christi said, when Oscar knocked on the door. He was wearing shorts, but ones that had been clearly used for work, as they were covered in splatters of paint, and a faded black T-shirt that had been similarly abused.

"No worries," he said, glancing around the kitchen. "Is Olivia out on the field already?"

Christi grinned and shook her head. "She's gone out for the day."

"How did you manage that?" Oscar asked with a grin.

"I'd love to say I planned it all, like some mastermind, but actually the situation just sort of fell into my lap."

"How lucky. I've got the wood, in my truck, and my tools. Have you got a spot for the fire pit, too?"

Christi nodded eagerly. "Do you think we can get it

all done today? It would be so nice to surprise Aunt Olivia – and get photos online as soon as possible, to increase the bookings."

"I reckon so, as long as you're not afraid of hard work."

"I don't know how much use I'm going to be, but I promise to work hard – and do as I'm told."

The day was warm but overcast, and the air was so muggy that by lunchtime, Christi's hair was a frizzy mess and she felt in desperate need of a shower. She kept her distance from Oscar as they worked, feeling a little uncomfortable with the mess she looked and how attractive he still seemed to be, even in a similar state of disarray.

They talked intermittently but most of their effort was focused on the task in hand. Christi held things in place, and hammered nails where she was told to, but had to leave the heavy lifting and the operation of dangerous machinery to Oscar.

Once the old shed had been fully repurposed into a new home for the shower block, they both took a step back and admired their handiwork. Christi grinned, and raised her hand to high-five Oscar, who responded enthusiastically.

"That was a great plan," she said, glancing up at the sky and wondering how long they had until Aunt Olivia returned. The clouds were looking rather ominous... The air felt ripe for a thunderstorm.

"Definitely doesn't look like an eyesore now, does it," Oscar said, wiping his hands on his paint-splattered shorts. "And once Olivia paints it – well, I think it will be quite an attraction. Maybe somewhere the young people will take selfies."

Christi gave a half laugh, half snort at that. "Are we so old that we have to refer to them as 'the young people'?"

Oscar cocked his head. "Well, you might not be, but I certainly am."

Christi batted his arm, in jest, then pulled away when she felt that familiar jolt at the contact. "Don't be silly," she said, to hide her blushes. "How old are you, anyway?"

"Thirty-three. Well, I will be next month, anyway."

Christi squirrelled away that information for the future. "I'm twenty-eight," she said. "So not that much younger. But I don't like the idea of being considered old..."

Oscar laughed and the sound rang out across the campsite. "Okay, okay. Not old. Come on, what's next?" Christi's stomach chose that moment to rumble loudly.

"Let's grab some lunch, I think we earned it. And then, if there's time, we could start on that fire pit."

"Well, you don't get impressive muscles without a bit of hard work."

Christi blushed, regretting the comment once again, and Oscar smirked.

The fire pit involved a lot of hard digging, most of which Christi ended up watching Oscar doing. After all, he did have the muscles. She brought him the tools he requested, and gave her opinion when asked – but she had to admit that the final product was far more Oscar's work than her own.

"I don't know how to thank you," she said as they

sat back and admired the fruits of their labour. "This all looks incredible. I'm going to go to the shops tomorrow and get marshmallows and skewers ready for the first campers of the summer holiday." She grinned.

"They'll love it," he said. "You've got great ideas."

"Just not the ability to put them into practice," she said with a half laugh.

"I'm happy to help. We make a good team."

He smiled in her direction, and she forgot that she was exhausted and aching and sweaty, and let her eyes drop to his lips, just for a second. There was something about him that was so tempting... And yet for all she knew, he had a girlfriend or even kids somewhere. He hadn't suggested any interest in her, aside from supporting her with the campsite renovations, and she was silly to jeopardise the easy camaraderie between them by asking him out. Or kissing him.

Even if both were on her mind.

The sound of a car pulling up made them both turn towards the house, and the waving figure of Aunt Olivia, in a dress covered in shooting stars today, made her way towards them.

"What have you two been doing?" she called out, and for a second Christi cringed, before realising her aunt meant the improvements they'd made, not the direction of Christi's thoughts.

"Just a few improvements," Oscar said with an easy smile. "It was all Christi's idea."

"And Oscar's hard work!" Christi chimed in, not wanting to steal the credit.

"Well, it looks amazing. Is that a fire pit?"

"Yep, and don't worry, it's got ventilation and I'll warn the campers that it's there – and not to let kids or dogs climb into it."

"And the shower block..." Olivia turned and faced the wooden structure. "How have you-"

"The concrete is still under there," Oscar said. "It's just had a bit of a makeover."

"That's where we thought a mural would be good," Christi said. "Maybe of the sea? But you're the artist."

"Oh, it's a wonderful idea." She clapped her hands together and looked up at the sky. "I'd start now, but I don't think the light will hold for long enough. Oscar, will you stay for dinner? You must be famished."

"Thank you," he said, his deep voice rumbling out into the warm air. "But I need to go home and shower, and I'm exhausted. But I'll take you up on the offer another time, I promise."

Remembering how sweaty she was, Christi was relieved she'd not given in to temptation and kissed Oscar.

"Yeah, I'd better shower too. Thanks for the help, Oscar – I owe you a drink sometime."

"What about Friday night?" he asked.

Christi paused. She hadn't expected to be taken up on the offer immediately, although she had certainly meant it. Was there any reason not to go on Friday? She would have one glass of wine, and there would be no chance of her acting on the silly thoughts that filled her head.

"Sounds great," she said, ignoring Aunt Olivia's pointed eye waggle as they all walked down the hill towards the house and Oscar's truck – and, more importantly, the very hot shower that Christi desperately needed.

"Those photos look great," Aunt Olivia said, her new laptop open at the table as they ate dinner together. Christi felt clean after her hot shower, but exhausted too, and she was looking forward to a very early night. She couldn't remember when – if ever – she had done so much physical work. "I didn't even know you'd taken any yet!"

Christi smiled and craned her neck to look at the laptop screen, which had the campsite's website loaded on it. "No point waiting," she said with a shrug. "If we're going to increase the bookings more, we need to sell the place."

"I just hope we can cope if the numbers increase drastically!"

"'Course we can," Christi said, helping herself to more spaghetti. The day's work had certainly given her a healthy appetite. "I'm here all summer. We'll be fine. Besides, I've got some more ideas... It's rather addictive, once you've started making improvements!"

CHAPTER FIFTEEN

By the time Friday rolled around, the bookings had increased significantly – and no one seemed to have anything negative to say. The thunderstorm came and went and beautiful weather returned, leaving the campers happily walking around with smiles on their faces and requests for more marshmallows.

"I don't think I've seen the place so busy since… well, ever!" Aunt Olivia said with a smile on her face as she returned from her usual morning round of the campsite.

"I'm hoping that's only going to increase," Christi said, a gleam in her eye. "The card machine should arrive next week, that'll make things easier. And I've got a couple of other improvements planned – don't worry, they're not costing much at all, and I've got it all under control."

"Oh, I trust you," Aunt Olivia said, and a warm glow filled Christi's chest. She didn't think anyone had ever said that to her before.

"I'm going to make some phone calls tonight, and hopefully it will all be in place next week…"

"You can't tonight," Aunt Olivia said. "Your drink with Oscar! Don't tell me you've forgotten."

Christi screwed up her eyes. "Is it Friday already?"

"You know it is. Now, where are you meeting him?"

She hadn't seen Oscar for several days as he'd been

at another job that needed him full-time for the week. Perhaps he'd forgotten about their drink entirely.

"We didn't agree a place," she said.

"Maybe he's coming to pick you up again," Aunt Olivia said.

"But then he can't have a drink. Doesn't seem very fair, really."

"Well, I can drop you down, but you need to know where you're going. Why don't you ring him?"

"Aunt Olivia..." Christi whined, feeling and sounding like a teenager.

"You have to get hold of him, Christi. You agreed to a drink, and he's a nice man!"

A very nice man... That was the problem. It was embarrassing to have to chase him up on the drink, knowing that her cheeks were flaming and her heart was racing.

"Maybe he thinks you agreed to somewhere. Or you've forgotten."

Christi grumbled but pulled out her phone. She couldn't claim not to have his number since she'd saved it in her phone after their beach trip. And her aunt was right...it would be rude to not acknowledge that they had made a plan.

Instead of ringing, she typed a quick text while her aunt filled the kettle.

Hey – just checking if we're still on for that drink tonight? No worries if you need to reschedule. Christi.

It felt weirdly cold not to put a kiss at the end of a text message, but it also seemed like it would say something.

Something like 'I want to kiss you'.

The reply was almost instant. *Definitely, if you still*

are. Do you need picking up?

I can get into town, just let me know where.

"We're meeting at eight," she called from her bedroom out to her aunt. "Satisfied?"

Her aunt said something under her breath and laughed, but when Christi went out to find out what it was, she wouldn't share.

"It's just a drink, between friends," she said, recognising that look on her aunt's face well. "And I might rope him into helping me out with my plans for next week, too."

The first thing Christi noticed when her aunt dropped her off was that Oscar was wearing a shirt. Not a T-shirt, not a polo shirt, but an actual shirt with buttons. Granted, it had short sleeves, but it was the smartest item of clothing she had seen him wear. And, paired with his tight black jeans, it made her mouth go dry.

"Hey," he said, his smile lighting up his face.

She wondered if she ought to have made more of an effort with her outfit – but she had thought they were going for a casual drink in a pub. She'd worn skinny jeans and a T-shirt, and she thought she looked okay, but certainly not as good as he did.

She was very careful, after her previous slips, not to say those words out loud.

"Hey," she said, raising her hand awkwardly in greeting.

"I thought we'd go somewhere different," he said, and she followed him, trying to keep up with his fast pace.

"How's the job going?" she asked. She tried to remember where he'd said it was, but couldn't.

"Oh, not bad, now that the weather's settled down

again. Don't want to be under all those trees when there's lightning forking in the sky!"

"No, I wouldn't think so."

"How's the campsite?"

"Busy," she said. "More bookings keep rolling in, which makes Aunt Olivia very happy."

"And it's all thanks to your changes and website," Oscar said.

Christi could feel her cheeks turning pink. Why did that always have to happen around him? He'd think she had a medical condition or something.

"Well, I think the good weather probably plays a part in it all," she said.

He hummed noncommittally.

"I've got some more plans, though," she said, and he turned and flashed her a smile. His eyes were bright even in the dusky evening, and she missed a step and nearly fell because she was distracted by him.

"Oh yeah, is that why you made sure we were going for this drink? Because you need my help?"

"No!" Christi insisted, although his help was certainly something she had hoped to discuss. "I've actually sourced several things myself this week – thanks to the good old internet. I didn't come here with ulterior motives."

Oscar stopped at a bar overlooking the water, and held open the glass door for her to enter.

"I can't promise the same," he said, and the words, and the anticipation, made her shiver.

She didn't ask what he meant. She couldn't. It was too embarrassing. Because it probably wasn't anything to do with the way her pulse raced when he was near, and then she would have admitted something that he had no reason to know.

And things would be awkward.

Besides, even if he did find her attractive, she was working with him, and then she was leaving at the end of the summer. It was hardly a recipe for success.

One drink turned into two and then three, and Christi found it harder to keep track of the words coming out of her mouth. It became far too easy to giggle at everything vaguely funny that Oscar said.

"Do you never want more?" she asked when he brought over another round of drinks.

He tipped his head to one side and frowned. "More... alcohol? Regularly."

She laughed. "No, I mean... More going on. More than this small town."

He sipped from his bottle of beer and regarded her thoughtfully for a moment.

"Was that rude?" she asked when he didn't answer.

"I don't think you meant it to be," he said, and Christi's wine-addled mind couldn't decide if she ought to be defending herself against something.

He took another swig of his beer, then glanced out into the dark night, in the direction of the sea.

"I love it here," he said. "And yeah, it's quiet in the winter, but the summer makes up for it. I couldn't imagine living anywhere else."

Christi nodded and took a sip of her wine.

"There's a lot going on in London," he said.

"There certainly is," Christi agreed, trying to keep control of her tongue on those pesky s sounds.

"Did lots going on make you happy?"

She hadn't been expecting such a blunt question, and she took far too big a gulp of her wine to give herself time to think, and then ended up choking on it.

"Are you okay?"

She nodded, not trusting herself to speak, and felt the wine rushing to her head. It was definitely time to slow down.

"I see your point," she said when she was able to speak again. She didn't want to discuss whether she had been happy or not in London. She thought she had been, before the disaster with her flat and her job. Did living in a bustling city make her happy? She'd always thought so... But then she was thoroughly enjoying her time here, in this little town.

When the bell rang for last orders, Christi was shocked at how quickly time had passed.

"Is your aunt picking you up?" Oscar asked as he held open the pub door for her.

Christi laughed. "She'll be fast asleep. It's fine, I'll walk it."

Oscar frowned. "Have you walked it before?"

"No, but it's Salcombe. I can't really get lost, unless I walk into the estuary."

"I'll walk you home," he said.

"You don't need to do that," Christi insisted, buttoning up her jacket and finding her fingers were not cooperating as well as they ought to be. "You said yourself, it's a half-hour walk up a steep hill."

"It's Salcombe," he said, mimicking her words. "No street lights once you get out of town, and very little signal. I'm not letting you walk back on your own."

She was about to argue again when he took her hand and began to pull her in the direction of the dark hill that led back to Sunset Shore Campsite.

It was hard to think of anything to say with his

strong, rough hand around hers, propelling her forwards.

She couldn't remember the last time she'd held hands with a man. That was something you did with a boyfriend, a partner, not on a one-off date.

Not out for a drink with a friend.

It was disconcerting to feel his fingers against her own, and yet warmth spread through her body from the point where their hands touched, and she couldn't make any sensible words come out of her mouth.

The hill was steep, and if he hadn't kept hold of her hand, she would have stopped several times to complain about how unfit she was.

But he didn't stop and so neither did she, until they were on the narrow winding lane that led to the campsite.

"I'll be okay here," she said, her voice a little breathless. She was very aware that their hands were still joined, and that she had no idea what he was thinking.

"I had a good evening," Oscar said.

"Me too."

A cloud blew across the moon, plunging them into darkness for a moment and then back into the eerie white glow.

"Good night then."

"Good night," Christi said, her eyes flicking to his full lips without meaning to. "Thanks for walking me home."

He still hadn't let go of her hand. She knew she ought to remove it, that she needed to go into the house and sober up.

And then he leant forwards and pressed his lips to hers.

Christi's heart began to race, her lips responding to his without thinking. Her lips tingled as his hand moved to her waist, pulling her closer.

An owl hooted in the distance, and Christi came to her senses.

She pushed him away gently, and he recoiled, his eyes widening.

"I don't think we should..." Christi said, her body still leaning towards him even as her mind told her she should be putting distance between them.

"Right," he said, dropping her hand and clearing his throat. "Sorry. I–"

"No," she said. "It's not..." She struggled to put her thoughts into words. She couldn't tell him that there was a part of her – a worryingly large part – that wanted to keep kissing him. She couldn't tell him how her whole body felt on fire from his touch. But she needed his help, she wanted his friendship, and she was leaving at the end of the summer.

Starting something romantic between them would just make things unnecessarily complicated.

But the hurt look in his eyes made her feel terrible. And her hand felt cold without his wrapped around it.

"Look, Oscar, I just think–"

He held up a hand. "Hey, don't worry. Too much to drink. I get it. See you around, Christi."

She watched him disappear into the darkness, half wanting to run after him, and half wanting the ground to swallow her up.

Things were finally going right with the campsite, and now she'd messed everything up.

CHAPTER SIXTEEN

Christi woke up with a terrible headache and a dry, fuzzy feeling in her mouth. It took her a moment to remember why she felt so rough – and then it all came flooding back.

The drinking. The walk. The kiss...

Oh god, the kiss.

She turned over and buried her head in her pillow, wondering if there was any way things could go on as normal today.

It was hard to work out what the mistake had been in her mind: the kiss? Or pushing him away? Because that kiss had felt good, she had to admit it. Oscar knew what he was doing. And he was beyond good-looking. Would it have been so terrible to wrap her arms around his neck, pull him close and see where the night took them?

She was leaving in a few short weeks. Maybe Oscar just wanted some fun, but maybe he wanted something more – and things would be complicated. He was a nice guy, and he had been so helpful, and Aunt Olivia relied on him so much. She couldn't mess all that up by sleeping with him and then disappearing back to her life in London without a second glance.

The thought of going back to London set her stomach rolling, and she was very worried for a moment that she was going to throw up the alcohol from the night before. It had been a long time since she had been drunk enough to throw up the next day, and she tried to remember just how much she had consumed.

She hadn't been aiming to get drunk, that was for sure – it was just so easy to sit and chat with Oscar, to sip wine and laugh and feel his leg knocking against hers whenever he moved.

When she forced her head out from her pillow and saw her alarm clock, she groaned again. Eleven o'clock. She had slept through most of the morning. Why had Aunt Olivia not pulled her out of bed to get on with some work?

Christi dragged herself out of bed and into the shower, turning the temperature up to scalding in the hope of washing away all of her regrets and confusing emotions.

Oscar was hot. And he had kissed her.

Why the hell had she pushed him away?

And would he want anything to do with her anymore?

She liked his company, for more than just the free labour he offered, and it would be a lonely summer if he didn't want to speak to her anymore.

Instead of a night of incredible, no-strings sex, she was left with regrets, worries, and a hideous hangover.

Although, she supposed she would have had the hangover however the night had gone.

As she worked the shampoo into her brunette locks, her mind started to race. Had last night been a date? And she hadn't realised? He was wearing a nice shirt after all, he'd tried to buy all the drinks, and then the hand-holding, and the kiss…

Was she so out of practice at dating that she hadn't even noticed that she'd been asked out?

Or had he just had too much to drink and given in to the moment, just as she had? Would he have pulled away if she'd given him a second longer to do so?

There was no denying there was a spark between them, although she'd thought it was just her who felt it.

It seemed she was wrong.

By the time she'd finally made it to the kitchen, fully dressed and in need of some caffeine, Aunt Olivia was coming back in for lunch, a smirk on her face.

"Good morning, sunshine," she said.

"You should have woken me," Christi said with a groan.

"Late night, was it? You look better than Oscar, he's been skulking around the place all morning. You two must have overdone it!"

Christi felt her cheeks redden at the mention of Oscar and she turned back to the boiling kettle, hoping Aunt Olivia hadn't noticed.

"Sorry for not being around this morning to help," she said, choosing not to continue the conversation about the previous night. "I'll work late, make up for it."

"I'm not bothered, Christi," Aunt Olivia said with a laugh. "I'm going to make some lunch, are you hungry?"

Christi's stomach growled in answer.

"I should get to work."

"Food first," Aunt Olivia said. "Then you can get on."

Christi nodded, not finding the energy to argue, and sat down at the table with her mug of coffee. She opened her laptop and checked over the website, as she did every day, before checking the emails for the campsite. Aunt Olivia poured some oil into a pan and turned the heat up high, as Christi's stomach continued to grumble.

She grinned at the first email and starred it to read properly later in the day, when her head was less fuzzy. It was a promising lead on a very cheap hot tub, and she thought it would be the perfect addition to the campsite.

She supposed she would have to ask Oscar to help her collect it… But she would cross that bridge when she came to it.

A knock on the front door made Christi jump, and her heart raced at the thought of having to face Oscar after their awkward encounter – but she was relieved to see it was just a camper.

Aunt Olivia opened the door, all smiles, and the middle-aged gentleman held up a tablet with a crack through the screen. "You don't have Wi-Fi at all, do you?" he asked. "My kid's downloads have all been wiped, I just need a few episodes of that dog show, whatever it's called, and then all will be right with the world."

Aunt Olivia laughed. "The campsite doesn't, but you're welcome to use ours. You can set it up to download and then leave it here, come back for it later, if you like."

After he had gone, leaving his device plugged in to charge while it downloaded whatever show he had been looking for, Christi sipped her coffee and wondered aloud.

"Could we give the campsite Wi-Fi?" she asked.

Aunt Olivia frowned. "You're the tech whiz, not me," she said. "Besides, don't people camp to get away from all the pressures of real life – including the internet?"

"Yes…" Christi said slowly. "But the phone signal is terrible here. They might want to check in on something, or watch something of an evening, especially if the weather's rubbish."

Aunt Olivia cracked four eggs into the sizzling pan

before responding. "If you think it's possible, I trust your judgement!"

Christi grinned and added it to her long to-do list. She had so many ideas for how to improve the campsite – she just needed to implement them all before it was time to go home.

"Thought you might need something substantial," Aunt Olivia said, putting a fried egg sandwich in front of Christi.

"You're a lifesaver," Christi said, the smell of the sandwich making her quickly shove her laptop away.

"I've done Oscar one too, let me go and shout him."

Christi paused just as she was about to bite into the sandwich and closed her eyes for a moment. She was going to have to face him, she knew that. She just hadn't expected it to be quite so soon, and in such close quarters.

She took a bite of the sandwich, unable to resist, then swore as the soft yoke broke and dripped onto her clean clothes.

And it was at that moment that Aunt Olivia reappeared, a sheepish-looking Oscar in tow.

Christi felt her cheeks flushing bright red as she put the sandwich down and fumbled to grab some kitchen roll, trying to wipe away the mess without it being too obvious. But her white sweatshirt was clearly destined for the wash, and her shame was written across her face.

"Hey," Oscar muttered, taking a seat at the farmhouse-style kitchen table and avoiding looking at her.

"Morning," Christi said, wondering if she ought to take the sweatshirt off or whether that would draw more attention to the mark.

"Afternoon, more like," Aunt Olivia said with a

laugh, putting a sandwich and a cup of coffee in front of Oscar. "You two must have had a wild night!"

Christi's head shot up and her eyes met Oscar's for a moment. His were wide too, and bloodshot, and he looked like he wanted the ground to swallow him up.

Just like Christi did.

"Was it a good night?" Aunt Olivia asked, clearly unwilling to let it go.

"Yeah," Christi said, pulling her lukewarm mug of coffee towards her. "Drank too much, though."

She watched Oscar as he bit his bottom lip before responding. "Yeah. Too much."

Did that mean he regretted the kiss? Or that he was embarrassed? Or was he irritated that she had said they shouldn't do it?

They ate their lunch in silence as Christi wished she was better at reading people, and had stronger self-control.

Christi managed to avoid Oscar for the rest of the day. She wasn't sure when he left to go home or off to other jobs, but she kept herself busy until she noticed his van was no longer in the driveway.

Lunch had been awkward. She supposed she shouldn't have been surprised. She didn't think she'd ever rejected someone's kiss before – well, she certainly hadn't rejected them and then had to sit and eat fried egg sandwiches with them, with her aunt watching on, clueless about what had happened.

What made it all so much more complicated was that she wasn't even sure rejecting him was a very good idea. When she looked at him in the cold light of day, without alcohol in her bloodstream, it was apparent that he was extremely good-looking, and she very much wanted to kiss him again.

So why had her drunk brain decided to be sensible and tell him it wasn't a good idea? That clever idea had only made things exceptionally awkward, and she hadn't even got a good kiss out of it.

She had plenty of time to contemplate her stupidity as she gave the shower block a thorough deep clean. The showers looked much better from the outside, but inside they were disappointingly lacking in power. She wondered if there was something she could do about that. Could she buy new shower units? That would require money, of course – something she didn't really have. And she certainly had no idea how to fit showers.

Oscar probably did. She was already hoping to ask him to collect the hot tub from a nearby village and help her set it up...

As she scrubbed stubborn stains off the wall, she rather thought she was asking too much. But who else was there to ask? She felt a sense of responsibility now and wanted to leave this place in better condition than when she arrived. She had never felt like she'd achieved much before, but if she left here having improved Aunt Olivia's business, even if she messed up whatever friendship she had been building with Oscar, at least she could look back on this time and smile.

Or at least, she hoped she could.

Oscar didn't return for a few days, and Christi didn't feel she could message him. Surely that would only confuse things between them, and she was already confused enough about her feelings. She found herself missing him, wanting to ask her aunt where he was, wanting to message him – and not just for help.

But then the logical part of her brain kicked in again, and she reminded herself that she was leaving in a few short weeks, and anything between her and the handsome Oscar was likely doomed to fail. If he even wanted anything. Which she doubted he did. Not anymore, anyway.

"I'm going to change the Wi-Fi password," she told Aunt Olivia over breakfast one Friday morning. "The signal boosters are arriving today, and once we've got a public password, we can share it with all the campers."

Aunt Olivia grinned. "I don't know what I'd have done without you this summer, Christi," she said, and a warm glow spread through Christi's body. "I've never had so many bookings for the August bank holiday weekend before. You know, I think we might end up selling out!"

Christi beamed. "I'm not done yet, either," she said, enthusiastically tucking into her breakfast. There hadn't been any more drinks out with Oscar, so she had no issue getting up early in the mornings to get on with her work. "I've potentially got some new showers being delivered tomorrow..."

Aunt Olivia furrowed her brow. "Can Oscar fit showers?" she asked.

Christi bit her bottom lip. "I haven't actually asked yet," she admitted. "But I reckon so. And if not, I've got a backup plan. Everyone around here is so helpful..."

"They are indeed," Aunt Olivia agreed. "I just wouldn't want them thinking we're taking advantage, using their skills for free just to earn more money ourselves..."

Christi shook her head. "They won't, I'm sure. You've given a lot to this community over the years and never asked for anything in return. Besides, it's not you asking, it's me. They are free to say no to me if they like."

"You haven't fallen out with Oscar, have you?" Aunt Olivia asked after a sip of her tea.

Christi swallowed, focusing her eyes on her plate. "No... Why do you ask?"

Christi saw her aunt shrug out of the corner of her eye. "I was just wondering. He's not been around as much as he normally is. Oh, he's getting the work done, of course – but he usually pops in for a cup of tea, has a chat... And you two seem to be getting on so well. I rather thought..." She trailed off, and as much as Christi wanted to know what her aunt had thought, she did not want to draw attention to it by asking.

"I'm sure he's just busy," Christi said, tapping her fingers on her mug of coffee. "It is summer, after all – lots of jobs for someone with Oscar's skills."

"I guess so," Aunt Olivia said, but the look in her eye told Christi that she was not entirely convinced.

CHAPTER SEVENTEEN

When Oscar came to the campsite to fix a broken fence, Christi knew she needed to talk to him. They hadn't spoken properly since that kiss, and she didn't want to destroy everything between them. Besides, she needed some help, and she didn't know who else to turn to.

"Hey," she said, squinting into the sunlight as she approached him, a mug of tea in her hand.

He stopped what he was doing and wiped his hand across his forehead.

"Hey."

"Thought you might need a drink," she said, balancing the cup on an unbroken fence post. "Hot today."

He nodded. "Hopefully it'll stay like this for the whole of August," he said. "The campsite will be heaving then."

"I hope so," Christi said. "Bookings are way up."

"All thanks to you, I'm sure," he said, his lips twitching into a smile.

"Us," Christi said, feeling awkward under his intense gaze.

"No more projects to rope me into?" he asked.

"Well..." Christi said. Part of her wanted to deny it, to apologise for the previous weekend, to not ask him for anything, but when he gave her such a perfect opportunity to ask.

"I've got a hot tub arranged, I just need to collect it," she said. "It's in a village called Goveton… I don't think it's too far?"

Oscar shrugged. "It's a bit of a drive, but not too bad," he said. "I can find some time this afternoon, if you like."

"Really?" Christi said with a grin, her awkwardness temporarily forgotten. "Oh, that would be amazing."

"Do you know how to set up a hot tub?" Oscar asked.

"Well, no…"

Oscar laughed and she was pleased to hear it sounded like his normal chuckle. "I thought not. Luckily, I've helped with a few."

"Thank you, Oscar," she said, wanting to throw her arms around him but knowing it would give mixed signals. "I really appreciate it."

"Although your aunt said something about showers…"

Christi blushed. "Well, that's not something I'm sure about yet, I–"

"I can't do those, I'm afraid."

Christi had begun to believe Oscar could do anything, and she felt her face falling before she had a chance to stop it.

"I can probably find someone who can…" he said.

"Oh, you don't need to do that," Christi said.

"Can't have you looking all disappointed," Oscar said. "Let me finish this fence, and we'll head out to get that hot tub."

As she headed back to the house to check what

needed to be done next, she realised she was going to have to spend the car journey in close proximity to Oscar, and she hoped it would not be awkward.

"I'm running an errand with Oscar," Christi told her aunt when she ran into her back at the house. "Is that okay?"

Aunt Olivia nodded. "Of course. There's a big group checking in tomorrow morning, if you're okay to be up to help? No late-night drinks tonight, maybe?"

She giggled and Christi cringed. She highly doubted there would be any more drinks with Oscar, and she was sad about that – but she couldn't tell her aunt that without admitting to *the kiss*. And her confusing reaction to *the kiss*.

"I'll be up, no worries."

She distracted herself, as she checked on some emails about the campsite, by thinking of the perfect position for the hot tub. There was a space surrounded by trees where you could see the sea, and she thought it would be amazing to sit in the warm, bubbly water, with a little privacy provided by the trees and a view of the ocean. Perhaps sipping a glass of prosecco...

What a great image to add to the website. And if the alcohol license she had applied for came through in time, they could sell the beverages themselves...

"Did you ask Oscar about the showers?" Aunt Olivia asked as she filled up the kettle. "I mentioned them, I hope that was okay..."

"Yeah, I don't think he can do them, but I'll figure something out."

"Well," Aunt Olivia said, drumming her fingertips on the counter. "I've actually got a friend who does some plumbing on the side. I don't like to ask him for help, but he did mention coming up to see the campsite, so I thought maybe I could..."

Aunt Olivia blushed and Christi gasped. "Is he a friend or something more?" she asked, a smile playing on her lips.

"A friend, Miss King, thank you very much. Do you want me to ask him?"

"Yes, please," Christi said, deciding not to tease her aunt any more, for now. She really did want someone to fit the new showers that had arrived, and she did not want to put any more pressure on Oscar.

"I'm making a lasagne for dinner," Aunt Olivia called as Christi grabbed her handbag and headed for the door. "Why don't you ask Oscar if he wants to join us?"

Christi pretended she hadn't heard and let the door close behind her without a response. She would see how awkward the drive was before deciding whether she wanted to voluntarily spend more time with him.

When she reached his truck, she didn't immediately see him, and wondered if he was still fixing the fence at the top of the field. She put her bag in the back, finding she had quickly adjusted to trusting that it was unlikely anyone would just walk off with unattended possessions, and walked around the truck to go and find him. But on the other side of the truck she almost fell right into a very present, and very shirtless, Oscar.

She put her hand out to steady herself and it landed directly on his bare chest. His muscles were solid beneath her palm and his skin was hot to the touch.

Without knowing how long she had been standing there, mouth dry, hand on his chest, eyes glued to his body, she suddenly became aware and pulled her hand away as though it were on fire.

"Sorry, I– I thought, and then, and–"

When she finally met Oscar's eye, he was smirking.

"What are you doing half-naked behind your truck, anyway?" she asked, forcing indignation into her tone to hide her embarrassment.

He did make her so flustered – and even more so without all his clothes on.

She'd been a fool to push him away.

"Some kid kicked their football into the fence, sent the tea flying all over me," he said. "I was just getting changed, before we go."

"Right," Christi said, hoping her cheeks were going back to a normal colour. "Yeah. Right. Okay. Well I'll just..."

She tried not to stare at him as he pulled a soft black T-shirt from a duffle bag and slipped it over his head.

When he opened the driver's side door and looked pointedly at her, still standing there gormlessly, she knew she needed to get her head together.

"So, does Olivia know about this hot tub plan?" Oscar asked as they set off on the main road out of Salcombe. Back in London, she would have thought this was a very small road, but she was sure the village they were going to would have lanes so narrow Londoners wouldn't even imagine driving on them.

Christi checked ahead. "No, it's a surprise."

"It's a good job she likes surprises," Oscar said. "I've got to hand it to you, though, these improvements of yours seem to be bringing the grockles in their droves."

"Grockles?" Christi asked with a frown.

"Oh, sorry, it means tourists."

"Didn't realize you had your own language down here," Christi said. "But yeah, it does seem to be working.

And I've got a great idea where we can put the hot tub, if you don't mind helping me..."

"I wouldn't be here if I minded," Oscar said, and there was something in his tone that made her feel guilty, even though she was not really sure why.

"I do really appreciate it," she said, hoping he could hear the sincerity in her words.

He nodded, indicated, and did not say anymore.

"Aunt Olivia has some friend sorting the showers, so I don't need you to find anyone – but thanks, for offering."

"No worries."

The conversation was notably stilted. She was going to tell him about her suspicions that there was something romantic going on between Aunt Olivia and whoever this man was who could plumb in showers, but she thought the topic might only make things more uncomfortable. Because if the other night had been a date, then she had simply rejected him – and he didn't know how torn she was feeling about that decision.

And if it hadn't been a date... Well, they had both drunk too much, both given in to the flames of desire that had been flickering between them from the moment Christi arrived.

Well, the flames had been flickering for Christi, at least.

"About the other night," Christi said, gathering up her confidence. Something needed to be said. She did not want things to be awkward between them.

"Don't worry about it," he said, with a nonchalance that sounded forced.

Christi took a deep breath. "I just thought... It didn't seem like a good idea. I don't want you to think..."

She couldn't seem to find the right words, and now they had passed through the town of Kingsbridge, and were starting down windy little lanes that made her stomach churn.

"Don't worry about it," he repeated again. "We were both drunk. What's done is done, let's not focus on it."

His words ought to have made her feel some relief, but they didn't sound sincere, and they left her with even more questions. Had it been a date? Had he planned it? Did he want to kiss her like she wanted to kiss him? Did he understand why she thought it wasn't a good idea? Or why she had thought that she thought that it wasn't a good idea...

She didn't really know anymore. Seeing him shirtless had sent her mind into a tizzy. Was she so shallow to give in entirely to sexual attraction without thinking of the consequences? The sensible part of her brain had won out the previous weekend... And yet now she could not help but feel some regret about that.

"How much are you paying for this hot tub, then?" Oscar asked, breaking the awkward silence between them.

Christi tried to rid her mind of all her questions and focus on what he was asking.

"Nothing, amazingly. It used to belong to a hotel around here, and someone took it off their hands but they just don't use it enough, so they just wanted it gone."

"Sweet. And where do you think it should go?"

It was much easier to talk about the campsite than it was to discuss that kiss. "You know there's those trees at the top of the field, where it overlooks the sea..."

Oscar nodded. "Yeah, I know where you mean – it's pretty perfect, although you'll need to figure out power..."

Getting the hot tub into the back of the van between the two of them proved to be more challenging than it first appeared. The old lady who was getting rid of it lived on a steep, narrow hill, and Oscar had to move his truck twice because it didn't fit in her driveway and blocked the road. After a local man and a farmer had sworn at him and hooted loudly, Oscar had been forced to hurry along the detailed hot tub instructions the lady was giving Christi, and suggest they got the damn thing in his truck as quickly as possible.

"You're trouble, you are," Oscar said as they drove back through the narrow lanes of Goveton. Christi was about to disagree when a supermarket delivery van came towards them, and Oscar had to reverse miles down a windy lane until there was enough room for the van to slide past. Several times he pulled into a passing place only to realise there wasn't enough room, and by the time there was, they were nearly back where they'd started.

"The joy of the countryside, eh," he said as he started driving back towards the main road again.

"I am not trouble," Christi insisted when it finally seemed their path was clear.

Oscar laughed. "You're always dragging me into something. You've only been here a few weeks and I've had two hangovers, spilt tea down my top, been sworn at by the locals…"

He trailed off, and she wondered if he was going to mention *the kiss.*

She was glad he didn't.

"Do you reckon we can get power all the way up to where the trees are?" she asked him.

"Going to add trying to get me electrocuted to the list?" he asked, but when she glanced over at him he was smirking.

"If it's not possible, you can just say," Christi replied.

"No, no, I reckon we can do it. The electric hook-ups for the campers aren't that far away, I'm sure we can rig something up."

"Something safe, right?"

"Are you suggesting I'm the dangerous one?" he asked.

Christi shook her head and rolled her eyes, rather enjoying this playful mood he was in. Maybe they could get back to how things were before. And she could imagine kissing him, with the knowledge of what his lips actually felt like against hers, but without risking some complicated situation that she was going to be leaving in a few short weeks.

The August bank holiday weekend was set to be the busiest Sunset Shore Campsite had ever seen, and Christi was thrilled to be a part of it. But then, once September rolled around, and the children went back to school, and the weather turned... Well, she would have to move back to London, restart her life. Find a new job, see if her flat was liveable in, and available, and if not find somewhere else. It was all rather daunting.

She pushed those thoughts from her mind. Today she had a hot tub in the back of her friend's truck, and her aunt's home-cooked lasagne to look forward to when she got home.

"Thanks again for this, Oscar," she said as Salcombe appeared on the horizon. The summer sun still filled the sky, even though dinner time was fast approaching, and she was excited to check out the view of the sunset from the spot she had chosen for the hot tub.

"No worries," he said. "It's been quite fun, helping

you make the campsite all la-di-da."

She rolled her eyes at his put-on accent.

"It's bringing the customers in, isn't it?"

"Yeah, it is," he conceded. "I guess I'm more of a wild camping on Dartmoor kind of a guy. No electricity, no hot tubs, no Wi-Fi, just the outdoors…"

"If I was ever to go camping, which I'm still not sure I would, I would be a luxury yurt, private shower and glass of wine in a hot tub sort of a camping girl," she said.

"Duly noted," Oscar said with a laugh.

They pulled up on the drive and Oscar killed the engine. "Reckon you can help me carry this up the hill?"

Christi grimaced. "Not sure I've got much choice. Aunt Olivia isn't stronger than me, I'm sure."

"I can find someone else tomorrow, I reckon…"

Christi shook her head. "Let's get it done."

"Better get a move on, before your aunt thinks I've kidnapped you."

"I thought I was trouble, not you," she said, hopping out of the truck.

"Yeah, well your aunt doesn't know that."

"Do you want to stay for dinner?" she asked as Oscar moved the hot tub to the edge of the truck so that they could get a good hold on it.

"It's fine, I'm sure your aunt isn't–"

"She said to ask you," Christi said hurriedly. "I just forgot. She makes a mean lasagne…"

"Are you sure you want me to stay for dinner?" he asked, and the jovial tone was gone, and his dark eyes were serious and sent a chill through Christi's spine.

She swallowed. Did she? Yes. Should she? She had no idea.

"Come on. Let's get this up the hill. Ready?"

Christi nodded and braced herself for the bulk of it. She was sure Oscar was taking most of the weight, but it was still a challenge for her. He took the lead, making rapid progress up the hill while Christi quickly got out of breath.

"You okay?" Oscar called, not sounding like the weight was causing him much difficulty at all.

Christi grunted, the only sound she was able to make, and their progress continued. Her foot caught in a rabbit hole and she felt her grip slipping. Her heart raced and she swore loudly. She couldn't smash the thing after all of this!

"Christi?" Oscar called, coming to a halt. His knee came up to balance the tub, as Christi tried to regain her balance. Her ankle stung and she hoped she was going to be able to walk on it.

"Sorry. Tripped," she managed to say.

"It's not much further. Can you manage? I don't think I can quite do it on my own..."

"I'm not giving up now," Christi said, getting her grip back on the side of the tub. "Ready."

It was slow progress, and Christi winced the rest of the way, but they finally made it to the clearing in the trees she had been picturing. And when she looked out over the sea, the sun starting to drop lower in the sky, reflecting off the calm waters, it all seemed worth it.

"Can you imagine it?" she asked Oscar. "Sipping a beer, watching the sun go down over the sea?"

He looked out over the sea and cocked his head. "I can see it might have appeal... To some people."

"But not you," Christi said. "You're too tough for something like that..." she added with a laugh.

"Let's fill it and connect it tomorrow," Oscar said.

"I've got to come back to trim a hedge that's overgrown, I'll help you."

Christi grinned. "Perfect. Then I can get some nice sunset photos, and we'll have even more bookings for the bank holiday…"

"But first, I was promised some amazing lasagne…"

CHAPTER EIGHTEEN

"Christi?" Aunt Olivia called as Christi was filling up the hot tub. She was worried the hose would retract and shoot water everywhere, since it was stretched so far, and so she was keeping a tight hold on it for as long as it took.

She cupped one hand around her mouth and shouted at the figure of her aunt in the distance. "I'm up here," she called, and was relieved when her aunt noticed her and made her way up the hill.

"Surprise," she said, when Aunt Olivia was close enough to see what she was filling.

"Goodness!" Aunt Olivia said.

"It didn't cost anything, before you ask. And I've cleaned it, and Oscar has connected it to the electrics. Soon we can advertise sunset hot tub sessions. I was thinking of stringing up some fairy lights..."

"It looks beautiful, love," Aunt Olivia said. "You've worked so hard, I hate to put something else on you..."

Christi frowned. "What's up?"

"Well, I've had a few guests come by this morning to say the Wi-Fi isn't working. You know I don't understand how it works, so I was hoping you might be able to take a look..."

Christi nodded. "Probably just needs restarting. I'll

come and have a look, as soon as this is full. I want to get some good photos tonight, once the sun starts to set. Let's hope the sky stays this clear."

Back in the house, restarting the modem made no difference, and so Christi spent her lunch break sitting on hold to the internet company, while adding to her to-do list. The showers – end-of-line models that had been heavily reduced – were sat waiting for Aunt Olivia's friend to fit them, so that was one item she could soon tick off. The alcohol license still hadn't come through, so she needed to chase that up, and she also needed to check what chemicals the hot tub needed. Then the marshmallows for the fire pit needed restocking, and the shower block needed scrubbing, and she needed to check if the card machine had finally arrived...

She wanted everything to be perfect for the big bank holiday weekend, which was less than a fortnight away.

And what she was going to do after that... Well, she didn't really have time to think about it.

"Has Oscar been around today?" Aunt Olivia asked as they ate their dinner that evening. Christi had been thinking she really ought to do some of the cooking – even if her food was nowhere near up to her aunt's standards.

"Yeah," Christi said, feeling the usual blush creeping into her cheeks whenever his name was even mentioned. "He helped me hook up the hot tub this morning, but I think he had somewhere else to be this afternoon."

Aunt Olivia nodded. "He's a very nice boy, you know."

Christi groaned. "Not this again, Aunt Olivia," she said, trying to stop her mind from wandering to that kiss, to her hand upon his chest, to the look of hurt in his eyes when she'd pushed him away...

"I'm just saying," Aunt Olivia said with a shrug. "You two seem to get on well."

"Mmhmm," Christi said, shovelling pasta into her mouth instead of answering.

"Perhaps, if there was something going on between the two of you..."

Christi felt her cheeks growing redder.

"Well, maybe you might want to stay. And that would be okay. Just so you know..."

Christi forced down a mouthful of pasta, nearly choking on it, and then took a gulp of water before responding to her aunt.

"I need to get back to my life eventually, Aunt Olivia," she said, sadness tingeing her words.

"I know. But if you wanted to change your life... Well, it's an option."

Christi blinked for a moment. She couldn't give up everything and move to Devon permanently... Could she?

"There's nothing going on between me and Oscar," she said instead. Perhaps it wasn't strictly true, but she wasn't going to admit to the kiss, or the way her heart sped up when she saw him.

She had built a life for herself in London. And yes, it had been falling apart around her, but she had never planned to give it all up. She couldn't live the rest of her life in a small town in Devon. She certainly couldn't move in with her aunt forever. And what would she do down here? The campsite was closed over the winter months and she wasn't going to sponge off Aunt Olivia.

"It's been a good summer," Aunt Olivia said.

"It has," Christi said, truly meaning it. "The best I

can remember for a long time."

Aunt Olivia smiled at her, her eyes a little misty, and Christi felt guilty for leaving her alone again when she went back to London.

"And I will definitely visit. I hear there's a really good campsite in the area…"

Aunt Olivia laughed and began to clear their empty plates.

"But I do need to go back. I left everything I spent years building in a mess, and I need to get it all back on track."

"I understand," Aunt Olivia said, stacking the plates in the sink and running the water to soak them.

"And if I was going to stay," Christi said, feeling like it needed to be acknowledged, "It wouldn't be because of a man. I would stay for you, Aunt Olivia, and the campsite."

Aunt Olivia dried her hands and reached over to give Christi's a squeeze.

Christi felt tears welling up in her eyes and she blinked them away, pulling her laptop towards her for something to do.

"I need to go up to the hot tub soon," she said once her aunt had gone back to washing up and the emotional moment had passed. "Get some photos while the sun's setting."

"It's a great idea," Aunt Olivia said. "Although we don't have many pitches left for the bank holiday weekend!"

"Well, it'll improve the reviews from the people already booked in, I'm sure. And next year, you should definitely up your prices."

"I don't know if I can run it like this on my own!"

Christi bit her lip. "I'm sure there's someone local

you could employ for the summer," she said. She wanted to say she'd come down again, that they'd have the same great summer the following year – but she had no idea what job she would have found in London, and how much holiday she would be able to take in one go. The whole six weeks of the summer holidays certainly wasn't realistic.

The campsite was fairly busy, and Christi wound her way through tents pitched across the field, saying hello to campers and stroking a dog who bounded up to her happily. A group of children were playing football in an emptier corner, and she found herself wondering if they could manage some sort of playground, or a swing set at least, to appeal to the families with young children. There were so many possibilities... And with so many bookings, and hopefully much higher revenues, perhaps Aunt Olivia could invest back into the business and grow it even more.

At the top of the hill, Christi took a moment to take in the sight. The field behind her, filled with tents and camper vans; before her, the ocean, with the sun casting an orange glow across the horizon.

She took in a deep breath and felt at peace.

It took her a while to get the photos she wanted. Ideally she would have had someone in the hot tub, looking out towards the sea, but she had no willing models and certainly had no wish to do it herself. Besides, she was the photographer, and although she had no experience with photography, she found herself very much enjoying setting up the perfect shot. Perhaps when her parents asked her what she wanted for Christmas, she would say a proper camera. Especially if she was ever going to do this sort of work again.

Maybe that was what she should be looking for

when she went back home to London, she thought. Some sort of branding work. Somewhere small, where she could get lots of hands-on experience, just like she had done here. Although she doubted anyone would trust her as much as Aunt Olivia had. And she did worry sometimes she had taken too much on. The showers were still waiting to be fitted, although Aunt Olivia had promised her friend would be round soon to do it, and while the Wi-Fi was working in the house, the boosters were not doing their job. The campers who had booked after she had advertised free internet had mentioned it a few times, and although they hadn't gone so far as to complain, she didn't like to let them down.

At the beginning, people had expected more than the campsite could offer because of Christi's social media skills. Now it was all there – it just wasn't always working as it should. She just hoped she could get it all straightened out before the big weekend. The weekend that she hoped would be the first one ever where Aunt Olivia had sold out of pitches. The weather was forecast to stay fine, at least. Christi had many things on her to-do list, but controlling the weather wasn't one she thought she could accomplish.

When she finally had some beautiful shots of the hot tub bubbling away, sunset in the distance, and a bottle of prosecco balanced at the side of the image (she was still hoping desperately that the alcohol license came through in time, otherwise the campers would have to provide their own booze), she turned to head back down the hill.

In the time it had taken her to get the shot, the sun had nearly completely set, and the picture before her had changed. Children were no longer out playing, and the fire pit was blazing, with a group of adults sitting around it, toasting marshmallows and laughing. Someone had an acoustic guitar and was picking out a tune Christi could not quite make out. The smell of a barbecue was in the air and Christi watched the happy scene with her heart full of joy.

She had brought all of this together.

She had never felt proud of herself before like she did in that moment.

CHAPTER NINETEEN

"Sam's fitting the showers this morning," Aunt Olivia called as Christi got dressed, having just got out of the shower herself. "So if you can clean them later, that would be great."

Once she'd thrown on some cropped jeans and a T-shirt – whilst wondering, since the weather was so warm, where her shorts were – she exited her room to find her aunt in a dress covered with tulips and her hair scraped up into a tight ponytail.

"I'm intrigued to meet this Sam," Christi said with a grin on her face as she made her morning coffee, not commenting on her aunt's new hairstyle.

"Christi…" her aunt said in a warning tone of voice.

"What?" Christi said, feigning innocence.

Aunt Olivia's eyes narrowed.

"You've been going on and on about me and Oscar," Christi said, feeling her cheeks warming even though she had chosen to say his name, "But I'm not allowed to say anything?"

"Because there's nothing to say," Aunt Olivia said. "Now, I need to check if he's got everything he needs…"

Christi laughed to herself as her aunt left. She wouldn't tease her too much, but it was too fun to ignore completely.

She glanced up at the clock. Normally she cleaned the showers and toilets first thing, but if she was waiting, she thought she might as well get some admin done. Bookings were going through electronically now, which was so much easier than people ringing up and her or Aunt Olivia having to write the booking in a big diary. Now if the card machine would only hurry up and arrive, everything would be much simpler.

There was a knock on the door just as Christi fired off an email to ask for an update, and she found herself rather hoping that it was Oscar.

Even though she had rejected him.

These feelings were very confusing.

But it was not Oscar's short, dark hair that she could spy through the glass pane in the door, and when she opened it she was faced with a smiling young woman, whose long dark hair fell loose around her shoulders in waves. She was carrying a wooden crate that was filled with cheese and milk.

"Hi!" she said, the grin on her face only widening. "I was looking for Olivia Noakes?"

"She's just out on the campsite at the minute," Christi said. "Can I help?"

"I'm from Colebrook Dairy," she said. "We've just started doing deliveries, so I've brought a sample crate, free of charge. We thought you might like to start a regular order – either for yourselves, or your campers," she said. "Miss..."

"King," Christi said. "But call me Christi. This is my aunt's place, but I reckon she'll be interested. Here, let me take that," she said, relieving the young lady of the crate and putting it on the kitchen table.

"I'm Ivy," she said. "My dad runs the farm, but I've taken over the shop side of things. Here's a card..." She rifled in the front pocket of her denim dungarees and handed Christi the slightly bent white rectangle. "If your aunt is interested, once you've tried our products, just let me know!"

"I will. Thanks, it looks great."

"So does this place," Ivy said, craning her head to look at the field packed with tents. "I've not been here in years. Didn't realise it was so... nice!"

Christi laughed. "It's had a makeover recently. Got a hot tub and everything now," she said with a proud grin.

"I'll remember that! Well, see you around, Christi."

Christi watched as Ivy climbed into a beaten-up silver car and drove off, then hurried back to the table to see what exciting cheeses were in the basket.

She couldn't resist going out to check on progress in the shower block by mid-morning. The ocean mural on the side of the building made her smile, as it always did, and she waved good morning to some of the campers before ducking inside to see how things were going.

The beautiful rainfall shower heads that Christi had managed to get hold of were lying on the floor, not in situ as she'd hoped, and there was a great deal of swearing coming from the far-end cubicle.

"Everything all right?" she called out as a screw dropped to the floor and rolled near her feet.

Aunt Olivia appeared, looking unusually flustered.

"Oh, Christi," she said. "Just a bit harder to fit than expected. Nothing to worry about!"

"Do you think I can get in to clean after lunch?" Christi asked. "There's a few campers who look like they're keen to take a shower!

"I'm sure it'll be fine."

There was a grumbling from in the cubicle, and Aunt Olivia disappeared back into it. Christi hoped this hadn't been a terrible mistake... The new showers were beautiful, but they were no use on the floor. At least the old ones had worked!

She tried not to panic as she went back to the house and made some cheese and pickle sandwiches. Had she taken on too much? They couldn't have no showers for the busiest weekend of the year!

But by noon, Aunt Olivia and the grey-haired, grey-bearded man who was introduced as Sam, both had smiles on their faces as they entered the kitchen to announce that the showers were ready.

"Amazing," Christi said, relief washing over her. "Thank you so much, Sam."

"No worries," he said, taking a seat at the table. "It's nice to meet Oli's famous niece at last!"

'Oli?' Christi mouthed at her aunt with a grin as her aunt put the kettle on.

"I'm not sure about famous," Christi said with a laugh, offering the plate of sandwiches to Sam. "But I am her only niece. All boys other than me!"

"These sandwiches are amazing," Aunt Olivia said, having taken a bite. "Where did you say this cheese was from?"

"A new dairy, I've got their card – this was complimentary, but if you want deliveries for yourself or the campers, they do that. It's pretty good, isn't it?"

"It is. I don't know how I'll keep track of all these changes once you're gone!"

A wave of sadness washed over Christi and she changed the subject.

"So, how do you two know each other?" Christi asked.

"Sam crashed into my car when I first moved here," Aunt Olivia said. "And after I was done shouting at him, we ended up going for coffee and becoming friends!"

"I'm not sure the accident was entirely my fault..." Sam said, reaching for his cup of tea.

"Let's not start that argument again, it's been going for a decade," Aunt Olivia said with a laugh.

Christi was desperate to know why they were only friends and not something more – and she wondered if she would be able to get that information from her aunt once they were alone.

Christi ought to have known, from past experience, that the good times wouldn't last indefinitely.

As she stared at the green water bubbling away in her beautiful new hot tub, she heard her aunt's voice coming from the bottom of the hill.

"Christi... Christi?"

Christi put her head in her hands. Please, dear God, she could not deal with another problem. With only a matter of days until the campsite was due to be the busiest it had ever been, the hot tub was green, she had no alcohol license, no Wi-Fi, and the electrical circuit didn't seem capable of supporting the sheer number of campers.

She had done this. She had built it all up, promised more than she could deliver, brought all these people to her aunt's door, and now, as usual, everything was falling down around her.

How could she possibly have thought that she could do this? She was just as much of a failure here as she had been in London, and as she had been at home, always shown up by her exceptional older brothers.

And now, Aunt Olivia was calling her name, probably to tell her of some other disaster that had befallen the campsite. Something else that was all Christi's fault.

She taped the sign she had made that stated the hot tub was out of order – although surely a fool would have realised that just by looking at it – and made her way back down the hill. She would have to face the music. She couldn't leave Aunt Olivia to deal with whatever problem Christi had inadvertently caused.

When she got to the bottom of the hill, her heart sank. It was indeed another problem, and one that she certainly did not expect Aunt Olivia to deal with.

But it was not a problem relating to the campsite.

Christi sort of wished it was.

"Mum, Dad," she said, forcing a fake smile on her face. "What are you guys doing here?"

Aunt Olivia was standing awkwardly behind them, looking a little sheepish herself. Had Christi's parents told her off for allowing Christi to stay here? That wasn't fair. It had been Christi's decision. She was a grown-up, after all, even if she felt like she was failing at adult life.

"Well, you've not been very easy to get hold of, have you," Mum said, with that disappointed tone that Christi knew so well.

"I've just been really busy," she said, waving an arm across the expanse of the campsite to illustrate her point. "Sorry."

"We had a bit of time off," Dad said, and Christi frowned at that. When had her parents ever had time off – let alone together? "And we thought we'd come down and see you, have a bit of a chat..." he continued.

Christi groaned internally. She didn't think she was going to like the outcome of this little chat... It sounded very much like code for a telling-off.

"Let's have some tea, shall we?" Aunt Olivia said, with a smile that looked as fake as the one on Christi's face. "You've come a long way; you must be shattered. Christi is staying in the guest room, but I'm sure–"

"I can sleep on the sofa," Christi said, filling the awkward silence.

"We booked into a hotel just a few minutes away. So don't worry," Mum said, and Christi felt a little embarrassed. There wasn't room to stay, but was that why her parents had booked into a hotel? Or was it because they didn't want to stay with Aunt Olivia? Not for the first time, she felt a rush of emotion at how similar she and her aunt were.

"It's a nice place you've got here, Olivia," Dad said once they were sitting around the dining table, with cups of tea before them. Aunt Olivia paused in her rifling through the cupboards to find some biscuits and shot Dad a smile.

"Thanks, Gerald," she said, finally finding a pack of digestives hidden at the back. "Christi has made a world of difference to the campsite. It's never been this busy before."

Christi couldn't help but smile, even though she felt rather awkward with her parents here, clearly intent on telling her what a mistake she was making.

"Well, that's all good and well," Mum began, tapping her long French-manicured nails on her mug. "But as we discussed before, Olivia, this is not the place where Christi belongs. She's got a life back in London, and

I – we – don't want her throwing it away to come and spend her days surfing and drinking on the beach."

Christi rolled her eyes. "Mum! I haven't been doing anything of the sort. And even if I had, it wouldn't be Aunt Olivia's fault. I'm a grown woman – perfectly capable of making my own decisions."

Aunt Olivia flashed me a grateful smile. "I invited Christi to spend the summer, and that's what she's done. Two adults making their own decisions. While it's lovely to see you, Emma, I don't quite understand why you're here. Now. It's not like you visit regularly."

Christi winced. Aunt Olivia was always so mild-mannered, and so to hear her speaking so bluntly was rather a surprise. There certainly seemed to be no malice in her words, but Christi thought she could sense hurt that her family never discussed.

Mum didn't respond to Aunt Olivia but instead turned her intense stare to Christi. "What about your job? If you'd come down here for a week, I'd understand. Two, even. But the whole summer – and what about your rent? Paying all that money for somewhere you're not even living in. It just makes no sense."

Christi took a deep breath. Clearly, some honesty was required – even if it wasn't something she relished the thought of doing.

"I was made redundant," she said, looking down at her tea instead of at either of her parents. "Nothing I did – just issues with the company, they had to downsize." Aunt Olivia would surely be disappointed in her for not having told them the truth from the beginning, so she didn't look at her either. This was more awkward than the lunch with Oscar after that kiss.

"Do you have anything else lined up? Did you get

decent redundancy pay, at least? Oh, Christi, you should have told us; we're lawyers, we could have made sure we weren't being screwed over."

Christi sighed again and kept staring at her tea. "I've not got anything lined up yet. I'll find something after the summer – but I did get a decent redundancy payout. And thanks to Aunt Olivia, I've not spent anything this summer – I've been pretty frugal since I've been down here, if anything." She dared to look at her aunt and smiled. "So I'm sure it will be all right." Mum seemed to be speechless, but Christi was sure it wouldn't last for long. She took a sip of her tea and waited.

"And what about your flat?" Mum asked. "You surely make more money in London, and if you're spending out on a flat anyway–"

"My flat flooded. The repairs were going to take months, so I let the lease go. I could have had a discounted rate, but I'd still have had to pay for somewhere else – and I just can't afford that. Even with my old job." Christi took a deep breath and then dared to look up at her mother. "This made sense, Mum, I promise you. I've had the best summer – and I've made money. Saved up money, even."

Mum looked at Dad, then Aunt Olivia, and then back at Christi. "So that's it? University degree, good job in the city, and you're giving it all up to live in Devon and work on a campsite?"

"Mum!" Christi exclaimed, frowning. "You're being rude." She glanced towards Aunt Olivia, who was being unusually quiet. "I never said anything about moving here permanently. I haven't decided exactly what I want to do because, to tell you the truth, I wasn't all that happy in London. Being here, making these changes at the campsite – it's given me some inspiration for what I want to do. I'll go back after the summer is over and figure out what I'm going to do with my life – but I don't need you telling me what I should be doing."

Silence reigned. Christi's hands were shaking. She had never told her mother exactly what she thought like that, never been so brutally honest with her. And it felt pretty great.

Just as the silence was beginning to get more than uncomfortable, there was a knock at the door, and Christi glanced up to see the familiar silhouette of Oscar Reynolds.

Her heart began to race, but there was a hint of panic there too. What would her parents say in front of Oscar? Would they talk down to her, as they so often did? She didn't want Oscar to see her as the failure that they did – even if he really ought to, after all the things that had gone wrong at the campsite. And she really didn't want him to look at her like they did.

Even if there was nothing romantic between them.

Aunt Olivia hurried to open the door, quite probably keen for an excuse to leave the table. Christi glanced up and tried to smile at Oscar, but she was finding it rather difficult to keep a smile on her face. She noticed too that he looked far more serious than usual.

"I think you'd better come," he said, looking at Aunt Olivia, and then at Christi. "I'm trying to fix it, but..."

Christi jumped out of her seat, not bothering to look at her parents. What the hell had gone wrong now? Clearly, something that was enough of an issue to ruffle the normally calm Oscar.

Christi and Aunt Olivia followed Oscar across the field – and the sight they were met with sent ice through Christi's veins. A woman ran screaming from the shower block. She was wrapped in a towel, but even that was soaking wet. A man hurried his two children away from the building with the beautiful mural – and even from a distance, Christi could see water seeping out onto the field.

She looked up at Oscar, her eyes widened in horror. "The showers?" she asked, hearing the door to Aunt Olivia's house closing behind her. Of course, her parents were going to witness yet another of their daughter's failures.

"They're shooting water everywhere," Oscar said, gesturing towards the building. "One of the shower heads fell off and nearly hit someone on the head. Everyone is fine – well, a bit wet and a little bit scalded or frozen, depending on which shower they ended up under."

"I'll shut the water off," Aunt Olivia said, her voice a little shaky. "And then... Oh God. I guess I'll have to call Sam and see if he can do anything. Christi, rope off the showers, will you, apologise to everyone, offer money off..."

She hurried off to shut off the water, and Christi watched dejectedly as Oscar hurried into the soaking shower block to try to minimise the damage. This was all her fault. She was the one who had pushed for the new showers even though there wasn't actually anything wrong with the old ones. And yes, it was Aunt Olivia's friend who had fit them – but she never would have thought of the idea if it hadn't been for Christi, and now, coming up to the busiest weekend of the year, they were going to be without working showers.

It was a disaster.

CHAPTER TWENTY

With Sam and Oscar desperately trying to get the showers fixed, Olivia rang around to find out what an emergency plumber would cost to get them fixed in time for the bank holiday weekend. The last thing Christi needed was to be cornered by her parents.

But they either did not realise how stressed she was or did not care.

The sight of her busily typing laptop did not deter them when they returned, having checked into their hotel and dropped off their bags.

"Is everything sorted?" her dad asked as they re-entered the kitchen without bothering to knock.

Christi sighed and put her head in her hands. "Not really," she said, her voice slightly muffled. "You know how it goes. Christi gets involved and everything is a disaster."

"That's enough of that nonsense," her mum said, folding her arms. "Running campsites, plumbing, no one expects you to be good at those things, Christi. Your degree is not in hospitality." Mum tapped her nails on the table to get Christi's attention. "Olivia will get it sorted, don't worry. She's managed the campsite for far longer than you've been here, and she shall continue long after, I'm sure."

Christi nodded then laid her head on the table. She

was sure her mum was trying to be supportive, but it sounded like the same old spiel. *Christi can't do it. Don't expect that of Christi. That's not where Christi's talents lie.*

But where did Christi's talents lie? She had thought she had been doing a decent job at the campsite. Bookings were up, the guests were generally happy – well, until today, when they had been faced with showers that shot boiling or freezing water at them and a green hot tub. There had been something at the bottom of a to-do list about chemicals – something she had clearly forgotten to do.

Maybe they were right. Maybe she couldn't do it. But then what did they suggest she do? Walk away and leave Aunt Olivia to deal with it? Go back to her nothingness in London, knowing that she was a failure in Devon as well as in the city?

"We are disappointed," her mother said, and Christi did not bother to try to conceal her groan. Of course they were disappointed. When weren't they disappointed? "We advised you against coming here, and you came anyway. You say you don't plan to stay here permanently, but you have no idea where you're going to go once the summer is over – which it very nearly is."

Christi wondered how angry they would be if she covered her ears and sang to drown them out. Oh, it was childish all right, but she was fully capable of telling herself how useless she was. She didn't need them doing it as well.

"However, we don't think it makes sense for you to return to London when you have no job or home there. So we pulled some strings and got you a job as a secretary in our law firm."

Christi frowned. "In Edinburgh?"

"Yes, in Edinburgh, keep up, Christi," her mother said. "You can live with us, like you have been with your aunt. Save some money. It's not cheap, but it's cheaper than London."

Christi wrinkled her nose. "I really appreciate it…" she began slowly. "But I don't really want to be a secretary. It doesn't relate to my degree, my interests, or even my talents – whatever they may be. I'm just not sure…"

"Christi," Dad said, a little exasperated. "What are you going to do? Stay here forever? Rely on your aunt? If you need taking care of, we're your parents, we'll do it." Christi didn't like the sound of that at all. She wasn't a child. She wasn't here for Aunt Olivia to take care of her. She was working. And okay, she'd made a bit of a pig's ear of it all. But did that really mean she had to go and live with her parents in Edinburgh? The thought was not a pleasant one.

"Let me think about it, okay?" Christi said with a sigh. "This has been a pretty terrible day, I don't want to go making life-changing decisions on a whim."

"Like you did when you decided to come down here?" Mum said, and Christi winced at her sharp tone.

"This wasn't permanent," she said coldly. "Now, I need to go and see what needs doing. Are you staying for dinner?"

Mum shook her head. "It's been a long day," she said. "We'll eat at the hotel, and come back tomorrow. We're leaving Friday – if you want the job, you'll have to come back with us."

Christi watched them go, unable to argue.

They wanted her to leave right before the bank holiday weekend. The biggest and busiest weekend of the year in Devon, and the one she had been working so hard towards all summer.

But what was she going to do otherwise?

She had some savings, thanks to the redundancy pay and the money Aunt Olivia had been paying her to work on the campsite – although now that would probably all end up going towards shower repairs and reimbursing campers for ruined holidays.

But that money wouldn't last long in London.

She didn't want to be a secretary... But she didn't know what she did want, either.

What a mess.

Out in the shower block, Christi was relieved to find that there was no long water spewing everywhere, thanks to Aunt Olivia locating the stopcock – but both Sam and Oscar were ankle-deep in water. The beautiful rainfall shower heads were on the floor, and Oscar was reinstalling the old ones.

"How's it going?" Christi asked in a meek voice.

"Better now the water's off!" Oscar said with a chuckle, and Christi was relieved to see he seemed to be back to his normal good humour. Maybe things weren't as terrible as they seemed.

"I don't know what happened," Sam said, fiddling with a bag of screws. "I'm sorry, I really don't know..."

Christi shrugged. "These things happen. As long as no one was hurt..." She watched them for a few moments. "Is there anything I can do?"

"All under control, love," Sam said, reaching out for a screwdriver which Oscar handed him.

"The old ones will work just fine," Oscar said. "And we'll figure out the new ones, once there's time. Maybe after the weekend."

When I'm gone and can't cause any more problems,

Christi thought to herself sadly.

"Thanks," she said. "Both of you – for fixing this. I'll go and put the kettle on."

Sam turned and grinned. "Milk and two sugars for me, thanks."

Christi left the shower block, the weight of the day heavy on her shoulders. If she left now, she'd never get to see how this all turned out. She couldn't put it right.

But if she didn't, she'd have no job and nowhere to live once the summer was over. She wasn't going to sponge off her aunt when there was no work to be done.

She turned at the sound of footsteps behind her, and saw Oscar jogging towards her, a grin on his face.

"Don't let this get you down," he said, and she felt as though she might cry at him being so nice to her. She didn't deserve it.

"It'll all work out in the end," he said. "Sam's a decent bloke. Although, between you and me, I think he was doing a little more than he was capable of to impress your aunt, if I'm honest."

Christi laughed, and even though she didn't feel joyful, she didn't feel quite as hopeless as before.

"Well, we can't blame him too much for trying to impress Aunt Olivia, I guess," she said.

"This isn't your fault," he said, when they reached the door to her aunt's home. "Just one of those things."

"I'm the one who pushed for all of this," she said with a sad smile. "I have to take responsibility for it all going wrong."

CHAPTER
TWENTY-ONE

One problem with making the campsite successful – no matter how much it was falling down around her now – was that there was no quiet spot for her to sit and despair. She needed a bit of time away from it all to figure out what the hell she was going to do. She couldn't leave her aunt alone in this mess, but neither could she turn down the job her parents had secured her without even considering it.

She needed money and security and right now she had neither.

With her parents at the hotel they had booked, and Aunt Olivia out placating campers, Christi left a note to explain she'd gone on a walk and headed out of the door, with only her phone and a hoodie. The weather was still warm, but darkness was falling, and she was sure the air would be cool by the time she came home.

She had no destination in mind. She just needed to think – and not run into anyone else she needed to apologise to. She made her way down the path to the centre of Salcombe, because it was the only route she knew, and tried to figure out how she was going to sort this all out.

How had everything come crashing down around

her so quickly?

She shoved her hands in her jeans pockets and sighed. It was the story of her life, really. Just when she thought things were going well, it all collapsed. Her flat, her job, now the campsite… This year had been rough.

And what on earth was she going to do to fix it?

They could cancel all the bookings for the bank holiday weekend. No campers would mean no complaints about the lack of facilities – including, if Oscar and Sam hadn't managed to sort it, nowhere to shower.

Oscar had said it would be sorted, but when she had snuck out for her walk, they had still been working on it. That didn't seem like a great sign.

If they did cancel everyone, the campsite was surely finished. Who would return to somewhere that cancelled bank holiday plans at the last minute?

Perhaps she could pay to fix everything that had gone wrong. She probably wouldn't be able to sort the alcohol license, or the Wi-Fi, but if there were working showers and the hot tub wasn't green, that would be a start.

How much of her tiny savings account would that use up, though?

Even if it used every penny, it seemed the only option. As long as she could find a plumber to come out and fix it. Then she would go and live with her parents in Edinburgh, work as a secretary, and try to save up enough to be able to do something else.

It seemed the only option. Christi the failure, striking again.

As long as she didn't drag her aunt down with her.

Christi was surprised to find she had reached the waterfront already. It was quiet, thankfully, and she took a seat on one of the wooden benches and watched as the boats bobbed in the moonlight before her.

She put her head in her hands and gave into the tears that had been wanting to fall since the hot tub had turned green.

She couldn't ever remember wanting anything to be a success like she had this campsite. For once in her life, it had seemed like everything was going right, like she could be proud of herself – perhaps even make her parents proud.

Not just be the forgotten footnote in the family tree.

Spending the summer with Aunt Olivia had been wonderful. She had felt at home in a way she hadn't done in years. And how had she repaid her aunt? By taking on far more than she could handle, and bringing her business crashing down around both of them.

She'd be unlikely to even be invited back for a holiday again.

And then there was Oscar. Oscar who had done so much to help her, and who she had rejected, hurt, even though every bone in her body wanted to grab him and kiss him.

Had that been a sensible decision? Or another in a long line of disastrous ones?

She was so lost in her own misery that she didn't hear footsteps approaching until a hand was placed on her shoulder.

She jumped up and went to scream, before realising that it was the tall, dark and handsome figure of Oscar with his hand on her shoulder. Quickly wiping the tears from her eyes with her sleeve, she tried to force a smile, but she couldn't stop another sob from shuddering through her as he sat down next to her.

"I'd ask if you were okay," he said softly. "But I think the answer is pretty obvious."

Christi laughed through the tears.

"It'll all be okay," he said, reaching over and putting his hand over hers.

Even in her distress, the touch of his fingers on the back of her hand sent a shiver down her spine.

"I've messed everything up," she said, looking down at his hand on hers and focussing on it. "Everything's gone wrong..."

"A few hiccups," Oscar said.

"People running from scalding showers is not a hiccup," she said. "This is classic me though. Disaster walking."

"Don't say that," Oscar said, squeezing her hand gently. "I don't believe it. And you've worked wonders on the campsite this summer. I've never seen it so busy."

"Yeah, even more people to complain now," Christi said with a sniff. "I took on more than I could handle, and now Aunt Olivia's reputation will be destroyed."

"She asked Sam to fit the showers," Oscar said. "It's not all you. And besides, people are quick to forgive when the sun is shining."

"Not when they're desperate for a shower," Christi said darkly.

"I've got a plan for that, don't worry. We might not have got it sorted today but it'll all work out. Why don't you come back to the campsite, have a cup of tea, get an early night. It'll all look better in the morning."

Another sob tore through her and she clung to his hand as if he were the only thing grounding her.

She looked up at him, knowing the desperation in

her eyes but unable to care.

"I don't think it will," she said sadly. "But I'm not going to leave Aunt Olivia in this mess. Even if my parents... Well, it doesn't matter. It'll have to wait." She bit her bottom lip. "I know I probably seem ridiculous," she said with a sigh. "But I've never...never wanted anything to succeed like I have this summer. Never put so much into it or worked so hard..."

She blinked, holding his dark-eyed gaze even though it sent a frisson through her body. "I've never thought something was going to be successful before," she admitted. "And now it's all gone wrong and I don't even know where to start."

"You're being way too hard on yourself," Oscar said. He reached up a thumb to swipe the tears from her cheeks and she shuddered and leant into his touch.

She knew she wasn't being fair to him, blowing so hot and cold, and yet she couldn't pull away from him now.

Without thinking it through she leant forwards and pressed her lips to his. It was only a moment of contact but it sent heat flooding through her. He did not pull away, but neither did he try to deepen the kiss, and after a minute she pulled away, feeling awkward and embarrassed.

Disaster Christi strikes again, she thought.

"I'm sorry," she said, pulling her hand away and standing up quickly, putting her hands on the stone wall and staring out into the pitch-black distance. "I'm sorry, Oscar. I shouldn't have... I just... And you..." The words wouldn't come out properly, perhaps because the thoughts in her head were so muddled.

"You don't have to apologise," Oscar said.

Christi whirled around. "I do, Oscar. You've been nothing but lovely since the moment I arrived, and I've treated you like-"

"You don't need to kiss me to thank me. I've not been helping you out in expectation of-"

"I know. That's not..." She shifted her weight on the balls of her feet, struggling to explain what was in her head. "I didn't want to kiss you to say thank you. I... I've wanted to kiss you. Just because. For quite a while now."

She could feel her cheeks flushing red, but he deserved this honesty. Even if it made no sense, even if she was leaving in a few days, even if it changed nothing. She did not want him thinking that she was kissing him because she felt she owed him something.

"But you pushed me away," he said, his intense gaze not faltering.

Christi bit her bottom lip. "I didn't think it was a good idea. I'm leaving soon. I was trying... Trying to be sensible. But I messed up. I'm sorry, Oscar. I told you, walking disaster. I try to make the right decision and it's still the wrong one."

"So you didn't kiss me back because you're leaving?"

Christi nodded.

"Are you still leaving?"

Christi blinked back tears and nodded again.

"Right," Oscar said.

As they had been talking, Christi had found herself moving closer to him – but there was still a gap, and one she would not cross. As much as she wanted to sink into his arms and have his kisses wash away all thoughts of being a failure, she still wasn't sure it was a sensible idea.

And Oscar clearly agreed.

"Everything will be okay," Oscar said. "I am sure

of it. We'll figure this out. And I know Olivia has been amazed by what you've done – a few issues won't change her mind. She's proud of you, Christi, and you should be too. She wouldn't want you beating yourself up like this."

"I can't agree with you on that," she said with a sigh. "But I should go and speak to her. Apologise properly, make a plan. Crying down here isn't going to solve anything, is it?" she said with a sad smile.

"No, it's not," Oscar said. "How did you get down here?" he asked.

"Walked," she said.

"I've got the truck," he said.

"How did you know where to find me?" Christi asked. She wished she could take back the words immediately. Maybe he had just been out and had run into her. Not everything had to revolve around her.

"I didn't – but this place is so popular, seemed like a good start."

"Thank you," she said as they reached his truck and he opened the door for her. "Can we... Can we still be friends? Even though I messed everything up?"

Oscar pulled her into a one-armed hug. It was only brief, and as much as Christi wanted to prolong it, she forced herself not to.

"You haven't messed anything up. Of course we're still friends. Come on, let's get you home."

CHAPTER TWENTY-TWO

Christi decided to meet her parents at the hotel the next morning. She thought this conversation was better between just the three of them – and she would break it to Aunt Olivia later in the day.

She had apologised to her aunt the previous night, and her aunt had reassured her that it would all be okay – just as Oscar had done.

And, after a less-than-good night's sleep, she had made up her mind on a few things.

She wasn't leaving before the bank holiday weekend. She was going to figure out a way to fix this.

But she also needed to take the job her parents had offered her.

It wasn't particularly what she wanted to do and it wasn't the place she wanted to be at in life as she approached thirty. But it was what was on offer. There was nothing else for her. And if she had to deal with her parents reminding her how little she could accomplish on her own for a few months or years... Well, she'd have to survive that.

And hope she came out stronger.

The sun was growing warm by the time she made it to the hotel. She had not walked so much when she lived in London, but she had no wish to ask her aunt for a lift that morning, and since public transport was practically non-existent, walking was the answer.

She had no idea what room they were in, so she had the hotel secretary ring up to them to tell them their daughter was downstairs, and then she took a seat in the lounge.

Mum and Dad appeared not long after, dressed in smart clothes that looked out of place in the seaside town.

"Good morning, Christi," Dad said, bending in to kiss her cheek. She could smell his aftershave with him so close.

"I thought we were meeting up at your aunt's place," Mum said with a frown.

"We were," Christi said. "But I thought it would be easier to talk here."

Mum nodded and took a seat on a soft, green sofa opposite.

"Shall we order some tea?" Christi suggested. "I'm parched. It's hot out there already."

"Did you walk?" Dad asked.

"Only way to get anywhere when you don't drive," Christi said.

"You could learn," Mum said, signalling to a waiter. "It's not too late."

Christi considered that while her mum ordered tea for them all. If she was going to live in London again, then there was no point. She wasn't going to drive in the capital city.

But how realistic was it that she would be returning to the city she had called home for the last few years?

She had meant to ring Leila for a while now and had

kept putting it off. And now she was even less inclined. Because she would surely have to admit that there was no way back for her – at least not for the foreseeable future.

And did she want to live in a tiny oven of a flat again?

She had got used to having a little space, to being able to breathe, to waking up feeling well-rested and ready for the day.

Her parents' house in Edinburgh was pretty big. Maybe she'd feel the same up there as she did down here.

She had to give it a go.

"I've been thinking about what you said," Christi said, once the tea had arrived. "About the job offer."

"I really do think–"

Christi held up her hand, begging for a little quiet to be able to finish her sentence, and she was surprised that her mother actually stopped speaking.

"I think you're right," she said. "I think that this job – and I do really appreciate you organising it for me – is my best option."

Mum grinned. "Excellent. Do you have things you need to collect in London?"

Christi shook her head. "I've got everything I really need here with me."

"That makes things easier then. We can leave–"

"But that's the issue," Christi said, biting her bottom lip. "I know you want to leave Friday. But I've committed to this campsite this summer, and I've put a lot of work into it – and no, it's not all worked out. But I don't just want to leave Aunt Olivia in a mess. I want to see it through – until the end of August."

"Christi, be reasonable," Mum said, picking up her cup of tea and taking a sip. "We have to get back to work.

We've already been away longer than we wanted to be."

"I understand," Christi said, even if she didn't really know why they'd come all this way, if they were just going to complain. "I can get the train up, once the season is over."

"The job had an immediate start…" Dad said.

Christi took a deep breath. Why couldn't her parents see that she was trying to do the right thing here?

"I'm not trying to be difficult," she said, telling herself to keep calm and not get wound up by their attitude. "I just need to do this."

Mum looked at Dad, then back at Christi.

"I'm sure Olivia can manage," she said.

"So am I," Christi said. "But I want to see this through."

Mum nodded. "Okay. Let us look at our schedule, see if we can stay a few more days until the end of the month. And if not, we'll arrange a train."

"I can sort it, Mum," Christi said. "I've been living on my own for a long time now."

As much as she wanted her parents to see she could cope on her own – although why she was bothering, when she had agreed to move back in with them, she didn't know – she didn't turn down their offer of a lift up the hill to the campsite. She didn't fancy it sober. And there was a lot of work to be getting back to.

She was going to make this right.

When they got back to the campsite, she headed for the house, her parents following her. She wasn't sure what they planned to do all day, but she could at least put the kettle on for them. And then she would sit down with Aunt Olivia and discuss where they needed to begin. With two days before everyone arrived, there was a lot to get done.

But when she got to the house, Aunt Olivia wasn't there. She left her parents and wandered into the field, still nervous about running into angry campers who wanted explanations as to why everything was going wrong.

All she saw, however, were happy faces.

And many new ones.

Her eyes scanned the field to find her aunt, or Oscar – and she finally spotted them at the top of the hill, by the doomed hot tub.

Except when she reached it, a little out of breath, it was no longer green. In fact, it was crystal clear, with inviting bubbles on the top and a bottle of prosecco on its edge.

"What's going on?" Christi asked, and her aunt and Oscar turned to face her.

"Hot tub's fixed," Oscar said, rather unnecessarily.

"How? And it's not tripping the power?"

Aunt Olivia shook her head, her eyes shining.

"Oh, Christi," she said, reaching out and grasping her arm. "Everything's going to be okay. Just like I said."

"But how?" Christi asked. "What about the showers? And the Wi-Fi? And will the hot tub stay not-green?"

"The locals wanted to help out," Oscar said, gesturing to the busy field. Christi looked more carefully. The shower block seemed to have a constant stream of fully-dressed people going in and out, taking fixtures and tools. Someone else she didn't recognise was wearing a high-viz jacket and doing something to the power generator, while the girl who had dropped off the cheese seemed to be filling up the marshmallow jars by the fire pit.

"I don't understand," Christi said, feeling rather overwhelmed.

"When I mentioned everything that needed to be done," Oscar said with a half-shrug, "a lot of people wanted to help out. We'll get this place sorted in time for the weekend, don't worry about it."

Christi gave him a watery smile. "I wouldn't have expected–"

"I know," Oscar said. "Everyone knows how much work you've put into this place. How much business it's bringing to the area. No one wants to see this fail – for you, or for themselves."

"I messed everything up," Christi said, looking to her aunt with another apology ready on her lips. "And now other people are coming in to sort out my mess. As always. I'm sorry, Aunt Olivia – and thank you, Oscar, for organising these people."

"Well, I didn't really–" Oscar began, but he was cut off by Aunt Olivia.

"You need to stop thinking of yourself like that, Christi," she said, her voice unusually forceful. "You haven't messed anything up. You took a leap of faith, believed in yourself, and this place – and okay, so a few things went wrong. You can blame Sam for that more than you can blame yourself. Silly oaf claiming he could do things he clearly couldn't to impress me."

She blushed. Her voice was softer now, and Christi did not believe her aunt was really angry with her friend at all.

Aunt Olivia reached out and grabbed Christi's hand. "You've made this place so much better than I had imagined it could be, Christi. I have let it carry on for years being half-empty with no ideas or motivation to improve it. You are a force to be reckoned with, love, and I am so glad you came and turned everything upside down. Even if a few things fell out along the way."

They both laughed, Christi with tears in her eyes, while Oscar looked on a little awkwardly.

Christi wiped her eyes on her sleeve. She needed to tell her aunt that she was leaving in a few days' time – which was a little earlier than she'd initially said – but now wasn't the moment.

"Okay," she said, Aunt Olivia's love and support washing over her and making her feel warm and more than a little overwhelmed. "What needs doing?"

Aunt Olivia looked to Oscar.

"All the physical stuff is in hand," he said. "The only thing left is the alcohol license, and that's not essential..."

"It would boost revenue though," Christi said. "If I go to the council offices, do you think I can chase it up?"

Aunt Olivia shrugged. "Maybe. They're in Totnes, I would have to drive you, but I just need to–"

Oscar pulled his keys from his jeans pocket. "I'll take you," he said. "I need to pick a few things up anyway."

Aunt Olivia beamed. "If you're successful, you'll need to pick up some stock, too! My wallet is in the house–"

"I can buy it, Aunt Olivia," Christi said. "Don't worry. This is all going to work out. I know it."

And for the first time in her life, she actually believed that it would.

CHAPTER TWENTY-THREE

Christi woke up early on Friday morning, her whole body tingling with anticipation and nerves.

She couldn't believe everything was ready.

The new showers had been refitted and tested repeatedly, and they worked perfectly. The hot tub bubbled away, not turning green and not blowing any fuses. She'd seen campers in it the night before, taking aesthetic photos of themselves with the sunset in the background to post on social media.

That had got her brain whirring. They needed a hashtag for social media, and maybe a few more photo-friendly spots. She was already envisioning improvements that could be made for the next summer...

Except, of course, she wasn't going to be around to make them.

She pushed away that sad thought and jumped into the shower, keen to get started on her list of tasks for the day.

Most of the weekend campers would not be arriving until later in the day, but there were a decent number – many with kids – who had the Friday off too. She'd put together welcome packs for every group with details of all the best sights, the beaches they should visit, and information about the bar that would be available for the adults of an evening. All the campsite's facilities were listed, and Christi couldn't help but feel proud of herself.

She'd taken a photo of the list and sent it to Leila, feeling guilty for not having been in touch more.

Wow, you've been busy! The response had been quick, and that had made her feel even more guilty for leaving it so long to contact her.

It's been a good summer! Christi responded.

That looks incredible. You heading back to London soon?

She'd hesitated in responding to that. The answer was a resounding no – but she didn't really want to put it into writing.

She hadn't even managed to tell Aunt Olivia what her plans were yet.

Going to head to Edinburgh for a bit. Try to save a bit of money!

I'll miss you.

Christi had sniffed, closed her phone, and focused on what needed to be done.

Her parents had decided they could stick around until after the bank holiday, but she doubted she would see them back at the campsite. Christi would be too busy, anyway, to play hostess – and they would have plenty of time together once she was living with them.

The thought made her groan, and then she felt guilty for that. After all, they were giving her a home and a job when she didn't have either. She ought to feel grateful. Not be dreading it.

Although it was earlier than Christi usually got up, the sun was already shining and Aunt Olivia was, of course, already up and dressed. She grinned at her niece.

"Good morning, Christi," she said, jumping up to put the kettle back on the range. "Are you ready for today?"

Christi pulled out a seat and took it, drumming her fingers on the table for something to do. "I think so," she said. "A bit nervous though…"

"I'm quite excited," Aunt Olivia admitted, bouncing on the balls of her feet. "You've done such a marvellous job, Christi. And we sold the very last pitch."

Christi grinned. It *was* exciting – but it felt like a lot of pressure.

"Did you go up to the hot tub last night?" Aunt Olivia asked.

Christi shook her head. "I did Wednesday night though."

"Wait 'til after dark tonight – Oscar's made some improvements, it looks incredible."

Christi felt the usual glow at the sound of Oscar's name. She needed to tell him she was going on Tuesday. He deserved to hear it a little in advance at least. Even though she'd already told him she wasn't staying past the summer. It was the reason she'd pushed him away, after all.

He'd really come through for her in helping to get the campsite ready for the weekend. Even after she'd rejected him, and then kissed him, and then cried all over him…

He really was a good guy.

She was going to miss him.

"Your parents are still around, then?" Aunt Olivia said, placing a steaming mug of tea in front of Christi.

Christi swallowed. Now was the time. "Yeah. They want me to go back with them, after the weekend."

"Oh," Aunt Olivia said. "I see."

"It's a little earlier than I was planning to leave, but not much," Christi said quickly. "And they've got a job for me..."

"You're not going back to London then?"

Christi shrugged. "I can't afford to, really. And there's nothing there for me..."

Aunt Olivia nodded. "I'll miss you," she said with a small smile. "I've got very used to you being here the last couple of months."

A tear came to Christi's eye and she blinked it away. "I'll miss you too," she said, taking a sip of her too-hot tea to try to calm her emotions. "But I've got to have a plan. And this seems like the best option right now."

Aunt Olivia pursed her lips, and Christi thought she was going to say more, but instead she downed her mug of tea and stood up.

"Best get started," she said. "Campers will be turning up from ten!"

Christi nodded. "I'll go make sure the shower block is gleaming," she said. "Show off those new waterfall showers."

She moved their mugs next to the sink and grabbed the milk to put it back in the fridge. It was a glass bottle, and she thought she recognised the label.

"Is that from that dairy that sent the basket of cheese?" she asked.

Aunt Olivia glanced over and nodded. "Oh yeah. The cheese was so good I thought I'd order some milk. I'm thinking of maybe setting up a little shop, having some local produce in it... You know, for next season." She smiled at Christi. "You've inspired me to improve the place even more."

Christi smiled but it was bittersweet. She was

pleased that her aunt was carrying on with improving the place, and that she was happy with all the changes they had made over the summer – but sad that she wasn't going to be a part of it any more.

That she wasn't going to be living in Devon any more, with neighbours who were surprisingly happy to help and milk that was delivered in glass bottles and the ocean visible from nearly every place she went.

She had always planned to leave, so why did it feel so hard?

She threw herself into the tasks she needed to get done that day, instead of dwelling on the fact that she would soon be leaving. She was intrigued to see what Aunt Olivia had meant when she had said that Oscar had made improvements to the hot tub, but she didn't go up there. After all, her aunt had told her to wait until after dark, and so that was what she would do.

She cleaned the toilet and shower blocks, as well as the washing-up facilities provided, until they were sparkling. She made sure the marshmallows were stocked by the fire pits, and that there was plenty of kindling and matches. Then she started to go around the tents, checking everyone was happy. How wonderful it was to see so many smiling faces. Several asked her about the bar, which was opening that evening. In addition to bottles of bubbly to enjoy in the hot tub, they had decided to stock some beers and some wines served by the glass, too. Nothing fancy, but enough that the campers would hopefully not want to go anywhere else. They could enjoy the warmth of the day, and then watch the sun setting over Salcombe with a glass of wine in hand.

She triple-checked that the showers were working, that they went hot as well as cold, and that the pressure was good.

Then new campers started to arrive. The largest number since Christi had come to stay. Money needed to be taken – thankfully, they were able to use the card machine that had finally arrived. Pitches were allocated, electrical hookups checked, and information packs handed out. It was late in the afternoon by the time the trickle of guests arriving slowed enough for Aunt Olivia to remember that they had not eaten since breakfast.

But it was thrilling to see the campsite so busy, to see children playing – although Christi still thought they needed more dedicated play space – and people starting their weekend early with a cup of tea in the warm summer air.

Maybe next year there could be a full café, as well as their little bar, Christi thought. But she was letting her ideas run away with her. That was up to Aunt Olivia – and any new employees she chose to take on for the next season.

Some campers got straight into swimming gear and lugged bodyboards and buckets and spades with them as they headed down to the beach. The weather had remained beautiful. In fact, Christi could barely remember a miserable day since she had arrived.

She had visited Devon before in the summer, so she knew that they did not have their own magical micro-climate. It wasn't always like this. But it seemed that fate had brought a perfect, beautiful summer – just at the right time to make Aunt Olivia's campsite a roaring success.

She wondered if she would have a chance to go to the beach again before she left. When she had imagined coming to Devon for the summer, she had looked forward to the space and the fresh air and the sea. And all of that had been there... But she had thrown herself into working so much that she had not really had time to enjoy it.

Still, she wouldn't change anything about it. Well... It would have been nice if so many things hadn't gone wrong. But perhaps she wouldn't have felt the same joy at it all being fixed just in time, if things hadn't looked dire for a time.

She wished she had given in and kissed Oscar in the way she wanted to, that she'd had one glorious night with him. It probably wouldn't have been fair, to either of them – but it was the only regret she would take away from this glorious summer.

CHAPTER TWENTY-FOUR

With every single camper checked in and enjoying their camping weekend, Christi ate a quick dinner alone (as her aunt mysteriously had 'plans with a friend') and then headed up to check out the hot tub in the dark. She was sure it would be in use – it was a very popular addition – but she wanted to see what Aunt Christi was talking about.

She didn't need to get all the way up the hill to see the fairy lights entwined around all the trees surrounding the hot tub. It was magical. A little oasis, overlooking the sea, with the sun setting into the still waters.

She walked a little way up the hill, not wanting to intrude on those using the facilities, and glanced out to watch the final moments of the sun setting herself.

She took in a deep breath of the sea air and felt at peace. Everyone around her was happy. This had been a success.

And okay, so she wasn't entirely looking forward to the next phase in her life.

She would take it in her stride and come up with a plan for what she *did* want. She wasn't even thirty yet. There was time, still, to turn things around, to not be the failure of the family.

Or just to be happy doing things the way she wanted to – even if it didn't fit with the rest of her family's ideas of success.

"You did it," a deep voice next to her said, and she jumped when she realised Oscar was beside her. She hadn't even heard him approaching.

She smiled, hoping the dusky sky was hiding the blush that rose to her cheeks at the sound of his voice.

"I think it was more of a team effort," she said.

"What are friends for?" he said and when she looked over at him, he was smiling. The orangey hues still clinging to the sky were reflected in his eyes and Christi felt warm and fuzzy as she let her eyes linger on his beautiful face longer than was really necessary.

"You're good at this, you know?" he said. "Marketing, I guess it is. You've got a vision, you know what people like."

Christi swallowed. "Thanks."

"So if you're thinking about what you're going to do, in the future – maybe it should be something like that. I know you said you were in advertising, but maybe something…more hands-on."

"You retraining to become a career adviser?" Christi asked with a grin.

Oscar tutted but the smile didn't drop from his lips. "No. I just… I love what I do. I didn't plan to do it, I just sort of fell into it, but it makes me happy. And I think you should find something you love, too. You've looked really happy, this summer. Well, most of it."

"You mean other than the time I was crying on your shoulder?" Christi asked with a forced laugh. It was awkward to say, but not as awkward as it had been to live.

"Well, yeah. Other than that."

Christi looked out to sea for a moment. "I'm leaving on Tuesday," she said suddenly, the darkness closing in around them, with only the glow from the fairy lights and the occasional glimpse of the moon to break it.

He didn't say anything and she was tempted to turn and check he had heard her.

But then he wrapped his hand around hers.

The warm contact of his fingers against her skin sent heat shooting through her. She didn't know if she should pull away, or ask him what he was doing, or...

But no. He was sober. She was sober. They both knew she was leaving. If he wanted to hold her hand, she was going to savour every moment she could get.

When he pulled her towards him, so that she was facing him, their chests just touching, she gasped. She looked up into his dark eyes, and as the moon came out from behind a cloud, she tried to read all the warring emotions within them.

"I know this doesn't make much sense," he said, his deep voice rumbling through her. "I know you're leaving. I know this is confusing..."

He sighed and leant his forehead against hers. "I'm going to miss you," he said.

It was the second time she'd heard the words that day, and these tugged at her heart just as much.

"I'll miss you too," she whispered, because it was true, even if it wasn't fair. Her whole body was alight at this close contact, and she wanted more, she wanted to kiss him, but she was leaving in seventy-two hours and...

He closed the gap between them, and his lips were warm against hers, and his breath minty, and she wrapped her arms around his neck and gave in to everything she wanted.

She felt as though the only thing holding her up was his strong, muscular frame. His broad hands pressed against her back, holding her tighter as their tongues met.

When they pulled apart to breathe, they were both grinning broadly. Christi's chest was heaving and her cheeks were flushed red but she didn't care. She'd been kissed before, of course – but she had never felt anything like that.

She never wanted to let go of him.

"So you're leaving," he said.

"I've got to," Christi said, sadness lacing her words. "My parents have found me a job and a flat... And I've got to get back to real life."

"This isn't real life?" he asked, taking one hand off her back to gesture around them.

"You know what I mean," she said.

She could feel his heart racing from the point where their bodies met and she was sure he could feel hers. 'What now?' she wanted to ask. Was this it? Because if it was, it was wonderful.

Would more just make it even harder to say goodbye?

Maybe. But it would be worth it...

"What's next on your to-do list?" he asked.

Christi tried to force her mind to focus on the world outside of this kiss and those arms and that body, to remember what she had to do that evening. With her aunt out, she was in charge, but most of the big tasks were done. She had planned to check on the hot tub and then...

"The bar!" she said. "I need to see if anyone wants to buy drinks. I can't believe I forgot. I'm sorry..."

His hands dropped from her back and she shivered at the loss of contact, despite the warm night air around them.

And then he reached down and took hold of her hand.

"I'll help," he said. "I used to bartend, when I was younger."

Christi beamed and tightened her grip on his hand as they began to walk down the hill. It didn't feel awkward this time, but she could not stop thinking about the fact that he was holding her hand. She felt like a giddy teenager.

It was a good job Aunt Olivia was out, else she would be reading something major into this development. Something that could not happen, since Christi was leaving on Tuesday.

Oscar had made the bar structure, which was really a table with shelves behind for glasses and bottles. When Christi approached it, she found plenty of people keen to come and order a glass of wine or a bottle even – and the card reader she had insisted they needed was very handy.

Oscar poured drinks and chatted with the campers and generally made the process much more enjoyable. They had advertised a two-hour opening window, but the queue disappeared before that was up.

"Want a drink?" Christi asked, reaching for a bottle of white.

"Go on then," he said. "And then let's try some of those marshmallows. I haven't toasted marshmallows since I was a teenager."

Christi giggled and followed him to the tree stumps around the fire pit that they had put there for seating. Most of the kids were in bed by now. Several other campers were sat around, enjoying the light and heat from the fire as well as occasionally toasting marshmallows.

Conversation around them was soft and happy, and someone pulled out a guitar and started to play some Oasis.

Christi smiled and leant against Oscar's solid form beside her.

He put an arm around her, and she rested her head on his shoulder.

She didn't want to ask questions or think about the future right now. She just wanted to enjoy this perfect moment.

Eventually they moved to spear marshmallows onto toasting forks. Christi burnt hers, but it still tasted fantastic.

"As good as you remember?" Christi asked, as she watched Oscar bite into the sticky sweet marshmallow.

He nodded. "Better, I think," he said, once he'd swallowed. "Maybe it's the company."

Christi blushed. "Or maybe they taste better accompanied by wine," she said with a laugh.

They watched the campfire crackle and send orange sparks into the air. Some of the campers were singing along to the man with a guitar, others were deep in their own conversations. Christi had lost track of time, but the air was still warm. Summer would soon be over, and this beautiful moment would be no more. Cold winds would blow and leaves would fall and she would be hundreds of miles away.

But for tonight, she was here, and Oscar was here.

And she wanted more.

She turned to him and pressed her lips to his

without warning. He didn't pull away, and without hesitation he kissed her back. She could taste the sweetness of the marshmallow still on his tongue, and the bitterness of the dry white wine.

Her fingers found the short curls at the base of his neck and she tried to memorise the feeling of him, the joy she felt at this moment, when everything had worked out and this gorgeous, kind, wonderful man was wrapping his arms around her.

They broke apart when they heard giggling, and Christi blushed and hid her face in Oscar's shoulder when she realised they had been kissing far more indulgently and for far longer than was appropriate in public.

There was no nastiness in the laughter of the onlookers, though, and Oscar laughed along with them, squeezing her hand and pressing a kiss to the top of her hair, without any thought at all.

Christi's heart leapt.

"Do you want another drink?" she murmured to him. She didn't want this night to end.

"I've got to drive home," he said.

She nodded. She'd forgotten that detail.

"I'll have a soft drink, though, if you've got one?"

"I have some back at the house..."

It was an invitation. He surely knew that. One he was entirely free to decline... But one she couldn't stop herself from offering.

"Your aunt might not want me popping in at this time of night," Oscar said.

Christi swallowed.

"She's out for the evening."

Oscar nodded and then stood, offering his hand to her as she did so.

Sexual tension simmered between them, as hot and unpredictable as the campfire they left behind them as they walked down to the house.

Christi opened the front door – which, as usual, wasn't locked – and double-checked her aunt wasn't home.

Then she turned to Oscar. She ought to get him the drink, she thought. Ought to at least go along with the reason she'd invited him back to the house.

"You know I'm leaving Tuesday," she said instead, biting her bottom lip.

"I do," he said, taking her hands in his.

"And you still want…"

"I do," he said. "If you do."

She pressed a kiss to his lips in answer to that, then took his hand and led him towards her bedroom.

CHAPTER TWENTY-FIVE

It took Christi a moment when she woke the next morning to figure out why she felt so cramped in the single bed. She'd got rather used to it, in the two months since she'd arrived.

But then she realised it wasn't just that she felt cramped. There was a warm, solid body beside her, and her legs were entwined with longer, stronger, hairier ones than her own.

She opened her eyes to find Oscar awake, staring at the ceiling, his arms behind his head and a smile on his face.

There was no point in worrying if her hair was a mess or her eyeliner had run or she needed to brush her teeth. She couldn't get anywhere without climbing over him. She couldn't even see her alarm clock. She had no idea what time it was, or whether Aunt Olivia was home, or...

"Good morning." Oscar's deep voice seemed to fill the room, and she glanced up at him with a shy smile.

"Morning," she said, in more of a squeak.

"I didn't know if I should wake you..." he said.

"What time is it?" Christi asked, realising in the excitement of the previous evening, she had not set an alarm.

"Nearly nine," he said.

Christi sat bolt upright, then remembered she wasn't wearing anything and pulled the duvet up to cover her chest.

Her cheeks flamed red.

"I need to – busy day, and–"

"I get it," Oscar said, sitting up and sliding out of bed without seeming to care that he was totally naked.

She couldn't help herself from watching him as he collected his clothes. Those muscles...

When he turned he was wearing his boxers and jeans, and she realised she was staring and abruptly closed her mouth.

"Do I need to sneak out of the window?" he asked with a smirk.

Christi blushed and shook her head.

"No," she said, even though her stomach was churning at the thought of having to walk out with him, making it clear to her aunt that he'd spent the night.

They were consenting adults, and yet she still felt very awkward about making it so clear what had happened.

"Let me just get dressed," she said, shuffling off the bed with the duvet wrapped around her and gathering some clean clothes. She wasn't going to send him out to explain to Aunt Olivia alone.

She slipped into her en-suite and dropped the duvet. When she looked in the mirror, the situation wasn't as bad as she had feared. Her brown curls were sticking up in odd directions, but nothing a quick spritz of water couldn't fix. And even though she'd not removed her make-up, it hadn't ended up all over her face.

The stubble rash on her neck would be harder to hide, however... She blushed at the memory of how she had become quite so covered and quickly dressed, fixed her hair and brushed her teeth. She would have really liked to take a shower, but she couldn't expect him to wait that long. And besides, she needed to be out on the campsite. There was cleaning to do and checks to be made and marshmallows to be refilled and...

Was she always going to blush at the thought of a marshmallow?

When she exited the bathroom he was fully dressed, more was the pity, sitting on her bed and checking his phone.

"Are you late for work, too?" she asked.

He grinned. "Nah. I'd planned to be here anyway, in case anything needed a last-minute repair over the weekend."

"That's thoughtful."

"I try," he said with a shrug. "I could have had that second glass of wine though, in hindsight."

He laughed, and Christi blushed. It wasn't like she had planned the previous night... Even though she certainly didn't regret how it had turned out.

She gingerly opened her bedroom door, butterflies filling her stomach, but was relieved to see that the kitchen was empty. Aunt Olivia was obviously already out on the field – as Christi ought to be.

"Do you want a coffee? Tea?" Christi asked, her heart returning to a more normal rate now that she knew she wasn't going to have to give any awkward explanations.

"If you've got time, I'll have some tea," he said.

Christi nodded and filled the kettle, which was

surprisingly stone cold, and put it on the range. Aunt Olivia must have been up for quite a while for it to have entirely cooled, and Christi felt a wave of guilt for sleeping in.

She grabbed cups and tea bags while the kettle boiled, not really sure what to say in the bright sunlight of the morning after.

She collected the glass bottle of milk from the fridge and set it next to the cups, waiting for the whistle of the kettle.

"Are you okay?" Oscar asked.

She looked over at him, leaning against one of the kitchen chairs, his brow furrowed.

"Yeah," she said, with a half-smile. "I am. Are you?"

He nodded and closed the gap between them. When he took her hands her heart began to race.

"Yeah. I am. I know you're leaving. I know this is a bit awkward. But no regrets, hey?"

Christi swallowed and then nodded. "No regrets. Whatsoever," she said.

He bent his head and pressed a soft kiss to her lips. Her fingers moved to his hair, just for a moment, and the kettle began to whistle.

Then a door opened, the couple pulled apart, and Christi felt her cheeks flushing bright red at the sight of her aunt with a very shocked look on her face, coming out of her bedroom.

"Oh. I–"

"You never sleep this late!" Christi said, her hand still on the back of Oscar's neck. She didn't know what else to say.

"I had a late night," Aunt Olivia said, with a hint of a blush in her own cheeks. "And I didn't realise I had to keep you informed of my schedule, *Mum*," she said, a wry smile on her face.

"No. Sorry. Course not. I was just surprised..."

"Mmhmm," Aunt Olivia said, her smile widening. "Good morning Oscar, dear."

"Good morning, Olivia," he said, and Christi's hand dropped from the back of his neck, allowing him to take a step back.

"I'd better get out onto the field," Christi said. "See you later."

And with that she fled, leaving the kettle whistling and Oscar and her aunt looking bemused.

She knew it had been childish to just run off, but she had plenty to do on the campsite, and she had been keen to get out of the awkward situation.

As she mopped out the shower block, she could not stop smiling. Sleeping with Oscar would certainly make leaving more painful – but today, it just added to her already good mood.

When she came out of the shower block into the bright August sunlight, the campsite had come to life. Children were running around, shouting and whooping. Parents cooked breakfasts on camping stoves while others packed up for a day at the beach.

The man who'd sat and played guitar the night before raised his hand in greeting, and Christi smiled and waved back.

Everything was good.

She checked on the hot tub – which was still not green, thankfully – and removed some empty bottles that had been left nearby.

She glanced out to sea and sighed. She was going to miss this view when she left. She was going to miss a lot of things.

Christi didn't notice Oscar approaching until she turned to walk down the hill and there he was, a mug in his hand. She blushed, and grinned, and ran a hand through her hair.

"Hey," she said.

"Hey," he said, a smile on his face too. "You not going to run away?"

"Sorry..." She bit her lip. "I did have a lot to get done."

"Uh huh... So much that you had to leave me alone with your aunt? When I'm very clearly wearing the same clothes as yesterday?"

Christi giggled nervously. "Sorry. Not good at awkward situations I guess."

Oscar rolled his eyes but he didn't stop smiling.

No regrets, they'd said. And Christi was determined not to have any.

"I brought your tea," he said, closing the gap between them and handing her the warm mug, handle first. "Thought you might need it."

Their fingers brushed as she took it and she felt a jolt through her entire body.

"Thank you," she said. The gesture was so sweet that she couldn't think what else to say, and so she took a sip and looked out over the campsite.

"Everything seems to be going well," Oscar said.

Christi nodded. "It really does."

"I've got to head out to another job in a bit," he said. Christi nodded again. Was Oscar ever not working?

"You won't leave without saying goodbye, will

you?"

Christi froze with the mug halfway to her mouth. "I wouldn't do that, Oscar," she said.

"I know. But I thought I'd better make sure."

"It's going to be a busy couple of days," Christi said.

"Well, it will be if this is going to be the roaring success I hope it is."

"I've got my parents round for lunch tomorrow," he said. "August bank holiday tradition. But I'll be here Monday. You know, if you need anything."

Christi smiled sadly and reached out to take his hand. She couldn't help herself. "Thank you, Oscar," she said. She hoped he knew everything that thank you covered.

When he had left, she took a moment to herself and sat at the top of the hill, looking out to sea. They needed to put a bench here, she thought, as she sipped her tea. The sun sparkled on the calm waters, and the boats in the distance looked as though they were children's toys, carelessly forgotten in the blue expanse.

Soon she would go and check in with the campers, and then she would face her aunt, and the inevitably awkward conversation that would follow. But for now she wanted to enjoy the beauty of the scene, the calm that she felt in her soul, the joy at everything working out the way she hoped it would.

And she tried to look at the positives of her future. Edinburgh was a beautiful city, and she would get a chance to explore it. That was one. She didn't want to live with her parents, to cope with them constantly pointing out her flaws or making out that she couldn't cope with simple tasks – but she would be saving money. And hopefully it wouldn't take long before she could afford to live on her own, and to have something bigger than a shoe box to her name.

Maybe she could even move back to London.

Being a secretary did not appeal to her at all, but she told herself she would use all her free time to find what she did want to do, and to secure a job in that field. She wanted to at least know what she *wanted* by the time she was thirty. Even if she wasn't doing it.

She reached the bottom of her cup of tea and stood up, ready to face the rest of the day. She would see Oscar again on Monday.

And then she would say goodbye to him on Tuesday.

CHAPTER TWENTY-SIX

"Goodness," Aunt Olivia said, as they waved off the last of the weekend campers. There were a few tents still dotted across the field, people who had taken holiday and could stay past the bank holiday, but the bulk of their guests had left.

And Christi – and her aunt – were exhausted.

Christi had been looking out for Oscar all morning. She had tried not to, but he had said he would be around on Monday... Although to be fair to him, he hadn't said when.

"I don't think I've ever worked as hard as I have this weekend," Christi said with a laugh as they walked back to the house, ready for a nice cup of tea.

"You've worked hard all summer, Christi. Not just this weekend. Thank you – for everything you've done. This place will never be the same again."

Christi grinned and followed her aunt into the house.

"I've got a list of other ideas, if you want them," she said. "If you want to do any more renovating over the winter..."

"I think I'll need a rest first," her aunt said with a grin, putting the kettle on the range. "But I'll take the list, thanks. Although I doubt I can do any of it as well as you can."

Christi sank into a chair with a sigh. "You know I've got to go, Aunt Olivia…"

Her aunt nodded and began to prepare the tea, in a teapot this time. Christi guessed they needed more than one cup each.

"What does Oscar think about you leaving?" Aunt Olivia asked.

Christi internally groaned. Her aunt had teased her a little about finding the handsome handyman kissing her in the kitchen, but the subject had mostly been left alone, since they were so busy.

"He knows I have to go," she said. "It… Us… It was a one-time thing, Aunt Olivia."

"Hmm," Aunt Olivia said, placing the steaming pot of tea onto the table, along with mugs and a glass bottle of milk. "I know you don't want your old aunt's opinion, but you two have had chemistry since the moment you arrived."

Christi blushed. "Well. Maybe. But that doesn't change anything."

If they lived in the same city, what would happen, Christi wondered as she sipped her tea. Would they date? Would they become something serious? Could she imagine a life where she woke up next to Oscar every day and crawled in next to him at night, exhausted and happy?

She could…but it couldn't happen. They were going to be living at opposite ends of this island they called home, and they both knew nothing could come of their one night together.

No regrets.

She was determined not to have any.

"What have your parents been up to?" Aunt Olivia asked, and Christi was relieved that the conversation had changed, even if it had moved on to a topic that never filled her with cheer.

"Mum said something about a spa at the hotel... But I wonder if that's just code for them sitting in the hotel room working," Christi said. "You know them."

"I do indeed. Workaholics."

Christi pulled her laptop towards her and Aunt Olivia frowned.

"Speaking of which, you're heading that way yourself."

"I just want to check the social media and the emails, see if anyone's left any feedback!" Christi said, defensively.

"Why don't you go down to the beach?" Aunt Olivia suggested. "It's a beautiful day, and you're leaving tomorrow. You should make the most of it."

Christi bit her bottom lip. The idea was appealing – but Oscar had said he was coming to the campsite. What if she missed him?

"I'm not sure," Christi said, focusing on the screen. "I need to finish packing, and to see–"

"If Oscar comes round, I'll tell him where you are," Aunt Olivia said with a grin. "And I'll help you pack this evening. You've not got that much, really."

Christi glanced at the clock on the wall. It was already nearly three in the afternoon... But a swim did sound wonderful, especially after such a hot and sweaty weekend. And although Edinburgh had beaches, the summer was coming to an end – and she rather doubted that the weather in Scotland would be as gorgeous as that in Devon.

This was her last chance to enjoy it.

"Let me just check these emails," Christi said. "And then... Okay. Would you mind giving me a lift?"

"Not at all."

Christi scrolled through the emails, getting rid of any that were junk and marking a few booking enquiries to check over later. The campsite was open until the end of September, although it wouldn't be anywhere near as busy, and she wanted to make sure her aunt understood the systems before she left.

Something else to check that evening, she supposed. She really ought to skip the beach and stay to get everything sorted, but it was such a tempting suggestion...

There were several notifications from their social media accounts, and so she logged on to read them.

She couldn't help but gasp.

"Christi?" Aunt Olivia asked with a frown. "Everything okay?"

Christi nodded and turned the screen towards her aunt. "People have started to review us, after the weekend," she said.

"Are they good?" Aunt Olivia asked, reaching for her reading glasses.

"Better than good," Christi said, a broad grin on her face.

Beautiful scenery, amazing facilities, and the owners couldn't do enough for us. Five stars.

We will be back! Luxury in the middle of such beautiful surroundings. Hats off to Olivia and Christi!

We've been here before and enjoyed the views, but the changes they've made are incredible. This is a luxury camping experience.

Christi couldn't believe so many people had already reviewed their stay. With that kind of response, she could only imagine the following summer would be sold out from beginning to end.

Tears filled her eyes, both from the joy of the comments and the sadness at having to leave.

Aunt Olivia looked at her, her own eyes damp, and smiled warmly. "They're all down to you, dear. You've turned this place around." She reached out and took her niece's hand. "Thank you. For everything."

Christi sniffed. "I should be thanking you. Taking me in for the summer, paying me when you didn't really need me, and letting me have free rein..."

"Our profits are through the roof, Christi. I need to up the salary I've been paying you. Or give you a bonus. However it works. I've been doing this on my own for so long, I'm not sure."

"You don't need to give me anything," Christi said. "I'm fine. That's not why I did this. I'm so happy it's all worked out. And you can put that money into more improvements – that shop that you mentioned, perhaps. And some of the things off my list, maybe."

"Well. We'll see," Aunt Olivia said, a twinkle in her eye. "Now, come on, you deserve that swim in the sea. And an ice cream, too. It's been a long summer."

It had been the best summer of Christi's life, and she knew she would remember it no matter where life took her next.

CHAPTER TWENTY-SEVEN

It didn't take Christi long to put on her bikini under a light summer dress and pack a bag for the beach. She wasn't planning to stay long, but she grabbed a book just in case. She had barely stopped all summer, and the prospect of time to herself with no expectations was almost daunting.

Aunt Olivia dropped her at a beach called North Sands, and, unsurprisingly, it was packed. Many holidaymakers had set off for home, with work the following morning, but the locals were out in full force, enjoying their extra day off.

But Christi didn't need much space. She found a small gap on the hot sand, laid out her towel, and pulled off her dress. After liberally applying sun cream – she wasn't going to burn on the last day of summer – she put on her sunglasses, lay down on her towel, and closed her eyes. It was glorious to soak in the sunshine, hearing the sound of seagulls, people laughing and joking, the waves hitting the shore, and the splashing of children in the water.

It was like paradise. She knew, of course, that it could not be this beautiful year-round, but today it felt perfect. It had felt perfect all summer long, truthfully.

Her relaxation was interrupted by a cold, wet football landing on her bare stomach. She screeched and sat upright, looking around for the culprit.

"Jamie! I told you to watch what you're doing. I'm so sorry. Jamie, say you're sorry."

A harassed-looking mother ran over, her shamefaced son in tow. He fetched the football, looking down at the ground, and mumbled an apology.

"No harm done," Christi said, even though her heart was still racing and she was sure she had made quite a fool of herself by screeching.

With another apology, the mother and son disappeared, and Christi used the edge of her towel to wipe the water from her stomach. Soon she would be ready to go for a swim herself; she wanted to make sure she was hot enough before plunging into the icy waters. It was just more enjoyable that way.

She glanced around, wanting to see if anyone was laughing at her for her ridiculous reaction to the football, and met the eyes of the dark-haired young woman she had first met at the door of Aunt Olivia's cottage.

She smiled and raised a hand to wave. She tried to remember the young woman's name. She knew she worked at the dairy shop with her father. She'd delivered the delicious basket of cheese. And she had been there helping when everything had gone wrong, and Oscar had engaged the help of a group of locals.

The young woman stood, her long hair reaching halfway down her back, and approached Christi. She desperately tried to remember her name.

"Hi!" she said, a warm smile on her face. "Christi, isn't it? I'm Ivy – from Colebrook Dairy?"

Christi grinned and breathed a sigh of relief.

"Yeah, of course I remember," she said. And she very definitely did remember the young lady – she just hadn't remembered her name.

"Gorgeous day, isn't it," Ivy said, sitting down on the hot sand next to Christi. "I knew it'd be busy down here today, but I couldn't resist. I just love the beach."

Christi smiled. "It's beautiful," she agreed. "I've got to admit I don't know the beaches around here very well. But I went to one last month... Thurlestone? I think that's what it was called. And that was pretty incredible, too."

"Oh yeah," Ivy said with a nod. "That's a good one. My favourite is Blackpool Sands. Have you been there?"

Christi shook her head. "I've been working all summer," she said with a sigh. "And I'm leaving soon. Well, tomorrow, actually." Saying it out loud to a virtual stranger made it all seem far too real, and a wave of sadness washed over her.

"Oh," Ivy said with a frown. "That is a shame. Maybe you could go next time you're down. I met my boyfriend on Blackpool Sands," she said with a shy grin. "I've always dreamed of getting engaged there, too. Don't you think that'd be romantic? A proposal on a beach?" She smiled dreamily into the distance. She was far more open than anyone Christi knew, and she didn't know quite how to take her.

"Yeah, I guess," Christi agreed.

"Sorry. I know I talk too much. I just say whatever is on my mind. I've always been that way. Dad is always telling me to stop and think before I open my mouth."

Christi laughed. "It's fine," she said, and found that she meant it. Ivy was more forthright than anyone else Christi knew, but she seemed sweet, and Christi imagined you got used to it.

"So where is home, then?" Ivy asked, leaning back on her elbows.

Christi had to think before she answered that one. Was it London? It couldn't be. She didn't have a home there or a job. Was it Edinburgh? She supposed it would be, soon... But it wasn't yet. She hadn't been there in a long time. She didn't feel any sort of link to it – aside from the fact that her parents lived there.

Was it here? Surely it couldn't be. She was leaving. This was Aunt Olivia's home, not hers. And yet... And yet it was the only answer that felt remotely close to the truth.

"That's a complicated question," she said with a half-laugh. "I might have to get back to you on that one. But I'm moving to Edinburgh tomorrow. So I suppose that will be my home. For a while."

"Edinburgh. How exciting. I've never lived anywhere but Devon," Ivy said wistfully.

"But you like it here, don't you? Even in the winter?"

Ivy nodded. "Oh yes. I couldn't imagine living anywhere else. Even if that does make me a bit boring." She laughed, as if the insult didn't really bother her.

"I don't think that's boring," Christi said with a shrug. "Knowing where you belong, where you want to be... That sounds pretty perfect to me."

She kept an eye out for Oscar the whole time, telling herself she wasn't, while she was talking to Ivy. When Ivy returned to her book, and Christi swam in the beautiful, freezing sea, she still kept glancing up the shore, hoping to see him. The cold water took her breath away, refreshing and shocking, all at once.

She walked back to the campsite, enjoying the view and appreciating those last moments of summer, and still she kept a watch for Oscar or his truck.

She didn't want to ask Aunt Olivia if he had called, but she told her anyway, seeming to know what it was that Christi needed.

"No sign of him, I'm afraid," Aunt Olivia said with a sad shrug. "It's not unusual though. He sometimes gets called out to another job and comes the next day instead."

Except the next day, she would be gone.

"Come on," Aunt Olivia said in a falsely cheery tone. "I need you to show me all that computer stuff. And then there's your packing to finish. No rest for the wicked, eh?"

It was at eight o'clock that evening, surrounded by suitcases that didn't seem to want to close, that Christi's phone beeped.

Sorry. It's too hard. Will come tomorrow to say goodbye.

She knew who it was from without even needing to read the name. A lump caught in her throat and she told herself she would not cry. They had said no regrets, and she had none – but that didn't mean she wasn't sad about saying goodbye. To him, to Aunt Olivia, to Salcombe…

To everything she had built here in two short months.

She went to bed that night with a heavy heart – and a message from her parents reminding her that the journey was long, and they would be leaving by nine-thirty the following morning.

"Thanks for having her, for the summer, Olivia," Mum said as Christi loaded her suitcases into the boot of the car.

She cringed at the words. She wasn't some kid who

had been taken care of for a few months. She was an adult – an adult who had done valuable work.

"She came for a job and she worked hard," Aunt Olivia said. "I would have been lost without her."

The pride that Christi felt at those words warmed her through.

She glanced down the driveway for the hundredth time that morning. She'd texted Oscar and told him what time she was leaving. Not because she wanted to make it harder for him, but because she wanted to say goodbye – and she'd promised she wouldn't leave without doing so.

When she heard the truck on the gravel, her heart leapt. Her parents both frowned at the truck making it harder for them to pull away, but Christi knew he wouldn't be there long.

"Hey," he said, raising his hand in greeting.

"Hey," Christi replied. There didn't seem any point in introducing him to her parents. After all, there was no reason for them to ever see him again.

"Morning, Oscar, dear," Aunt Olivia said, her voice warm.

"Just came to say bye," Oscar said, his hands in his jeans pockets.

When Christi had imagined their parting – which she had tried not to do very often – she had imagined them alone. Being surrounded by awkward onlookers was torture.

"Bye, Oscar," she said with a sad smile. She took a step towards him, and he towards her, and then he engulfed her in a hug that was too tight and too long and altogether perfect.

Tears welled in her eyes but she wouldn't let them fall. This was her decision. It was for the best.

Her father cleared his throat. "It's a long drive back to Edinburgh, Christina."

Reluctantly, Christi pulled away from Oscar's warm embrace.

"Let me know how things go, yeah?" she said softly. "Someone needs to make sure Aunt Olivia doesn't take down the Wi-Fi for the whole of the South Hams."

Oscar laughed and nodded. "Good luck up there."

Christi turned to her aunt, who was openly crying, and pulled her into a hug. They'd said everything that needed to be said, and so they just held each other, until Christi could feel her impatient parents' stares boring into her back.

"See you soon, yeah?" Christi said.

Aunt Olivia nodded.

Mum and Dad got into the car, with a pointed look at Christi, who opened the back door, feeling more like a kid than she had done in a long time.

"Wait–"

Christi's hand froze on the car door and she turned her head to look back at her aunt.

"Don't go," Aunt Olivia said, stepping forwards. "Stay. You have a home here, and a job, for as long as you want."

"Aunt Olivia," Christi said, her eyes wide. "The season's nearly over, you won't need–"

"You were right," Aunt Olivia said. "I didn't need any more staff at the beginning of the summer. But you've turned everything around so that there's no way I can run this place on my own any more. I could hire someone, but I'd much rather have you here. It's your life, sweetheart, and you must make your own decisions. But if you want a job and a home then you have one. Here."

The front door of the car had opened halfway through Aunt Olivia's speech, and Christi's mother stood there, glowering at her sister.

"Olivia," she said, her voice strained, her jaw tight. "Christi needs to think of her career. Being here will not lead her anywhere. Look at–"

"Mum!" Christi exclaimed.

"It's okay, Christi," Aunt Olivia said. "Look at me, that's what you were going to say, Emma, wasn't it? Well, I may not have your big car or your nice house, but I'm happy. I love living here, and I love my campsite, and I have seen how happy Christi has been here. So if she wants to stay – I want her to know it's an option."

"Thank you," Christi said, turning back to her aunt. "But in the winter..."

"There's plenty of improvements we can make," Aunt Olivia said. "Especially with all the money you brought in this summer. I have plenty of work for you all year, don't I, Oscar?"

Somehow she had almost forgotten that Oscar was there. His cheeks reddened at being pulled into the family row but he nodded. "Yeah. Plenty of work."

"I think you could be happy here, Christi. Build something you're proud of..."

"You can have a career in Edinburgh, Christi. Make something of yourself. You don't want to be stuck down here–" Mum said, talking over the top of Aunt Olivia.

"I don't want to be a secretary," Christi said, taking a deep breath. "I don't know if there's much point in making something out of myself in a career I know I'm going to hate..."

"You'll end up stuck down here with no prospects, Christi," her Dad said. She hadn't even noticed him getting out of the car. "There's nothing here for you. Leave this as a nice summer of memories and come back to the real world."

Christi swallowed. Was there anything here for her? There was Aunt Olivia. There was the campsite. And there was Oscar...

CHAPTER TWENTY-EIGHT

"Are you sure I wouldn't just be a burden on you, Aunt Olivia?" Christi asked, her heart daring to hope in a future that she actually wanted.

Her parents said she needed to return to the real world.

And she had thought that, too.

But why couldn't this be her reality?

"There's enough work. Longer hours in the season, less in the winter – but it averages out. And I won't charge you rent, either. I can help you find somewhere of your own, if you want... It's totally up to you."

Christi swallowed. It wasn't what she'd planned for her life. She had no idea if it would work out. But what she wanted was to keep building up the campsite. Maybe take on other businesses, help them to improve, market them better...

She wanted to stay in Devon. For the time being, at least.

She glanced at Oscar. How would he react? They'd slept together under the expectation that she was leaving. Would he be pleased that she was staying? Or was it putting pressure on him when he'd expected none?

He gave her a smile and a half-shrug that seemed to

say *'it's up to you.'*

She took a deep, steadying breath and turned to her parents.

She wanted to make something of herself. She wanted to do something she loved. She wanted to feel proud of herself.

And this summer she had, for the first time ever.

"I'm sorry Mum, Dad," she said. "I really appreciate the job and the home and I know you want what's best for me... But I think this is where I need to be. Here. In Devon."

"You can't expect us to come back and pick up the pieces when this all goes wrong," Mum said. Christi winced at her harsh words. Why did they always have to assume the worst? She tried to tell herself again that they were only looking out for her, but it wasn't always easy to believe.

She pulled herself up to her full height and nodded. "I won't. I'm a big girl. I'll be fine."

Oscar had moved his truck so her parents could get away easily, once Christi had removed her suitcases from the boot.

He hadn't come back, and she'd tried not to dwell on it. If things were going to happen between them, now that she was staying, then they would. And if they weren't... Well, she could live with that. She had never made a decision in her life based on a man. She had chosen to stay for herself. He was just an added bonus.

"I hope I've not caused a huge rift between you and your parents," Aunt Olivia said as they sat on the old metal table in the garden, looking out over the field with a mug of tea in front of each of them.

"They'll get over it," Christi said.

"I'm sure they just want what's best for you..."

"Yeah, I tell myself that," Christi said with a sigh. "But you're right. I've been happy here. So why the hell would I want to leave?"

Aunt Olivia beamed and reached across to give Christi's hand a squeeze.

"I wanted you to make your own choice. But I am very glad that you're staying. Together, I think we can make this place something really special."

Christi nodded. "I do too. But it's your business, your home – you must promise to tell me if I become more of a hindrance than a help."

"I don't think that will happen, but I promise I'll tell you. And you know, it's your home too. If you want to bring anyone over, Oscar, for example... There's no need to hide him. You're a grown-up – something your parents seem to forget."

Christi blushed and looked down at her milky tea. "I'm not sure... If there's anything between us. Long-term, I mean."

Aunt Olivia frowned. "Has he said–"

Christi shook her head. "We haven't spoken. You saw it – I said I was staying, he moved his truck, and that's that. It's okay," she added when Aunt Olivia went to speak again. "I – I like him. I'm willing to admit that. And I think he knows that, too. But I didn't stay here for him. So if he doesn't want anything more, it doesn't change my plan. I stayed here for the campsite, for you... And for me. And everything else... Well, I guess we'll see what happens."

Hoping to try out the hot tub, and thinking she might get a chance once her tasks for the evening were finished, Christi put on her bikini under a T-shirt dress before heading back onto the campsite.

She opened their little bar – which she hoped to expand the following summer – for an hour, giving the remaining campers a chance to get a drink and enjoy the end of summer sunshine. It was mainly adults on the campsite now, and a couple of very small children. She supposed most kids were getting ready to go back to school. September had always felt like such a time of great change and new beginnings when she was younger, and this year she rather thought it was going to feel similar.

She poured herself a generous glass of white wine and glanced up at her favourite spot. For the first time in days, it looked empty. She ascended the hill, glancing out over the sea with a grin on her face. It was the perfect time. The sun was setting, the air was still warm, and she was going to savour the perfect moment.

She balanced her glass of wine on the side of the hot tub, stripped off her dress and climbed in, sinking into the warm, bubbly water. No wonder this had been so popular with the campers. It was bliss. After the day she'd had – the arguments, the questions, the sadness, and then the joy – it was just what she needed.

When she heard footsteps approaching, she opened her eyes, scolding herself. She wasn't a guest. It wouldn't be right for her to hog the hot tub if campers wanted to use it. But it was so lovely, and the water so warm...

She turned her head, an apology ready on her lips, and her heart froze at the sight of Oscar. He was silhouetted against the setting sun behind him, and he looked as breathtakingly handsome as ever.

"You're staying then," he said, fixing her with that intense look that made her shiver in spite of the warm water.

She nodded. "Looks like it," she said, giving a half-laugh. "Don't think my parents are going to take me back in a hurry, anyway."

He smiled. The air was thick with unasked questions and unspoken answers, and Christi didn't really know where to start. She wanted him to know that this didn't have to be anything. That their one night together could just be one night – if that was what he wanted. But if he wanted more... Well, then she did too.

"Can I join you?" he asked, breaking the silence.

"I'm not sure you ought to be skinny-dipping, even if you do work here. I am meant to be in charge..." Christi's eyes widened, and her cheeks flushed bright red as she realised that, once again, she had said something in front of Oscar that was only meant to be in her head.

But he just laughed, pulled off his T-shirt, shoes and socks, and climbed in, still wearing his shorts.

Christi was very aware of how close he was and that she was only wearing a bikini and that her mind was swirling in ways she did not think she could blame entirely on the wine.

"Is it okay that I'm staying?" she asked as he leaned back in the water.

He cocked his head as he looked at her. "Of course it is."

"I just mean... I know I said I was leaving. And I don't want you to think that because I'm staying it has to lead to... Not if you don't want..."

Christi was aware she was babbling, but she didn't

seem to be able to control her words. She hadn't been able to since the first time she had met Oscar.

"I want," Oscar said clearly, cutting across her.

Her heart felt like it might jump from her chest.

"If you do, that is."

She grinned, and instead of answering with words, she leaned forward and pressed her lips softly to his as the sun set over Salcombe.

* * *

Will Ivy get her romantic proposal on Blackpool Sands? Find out in book two, available to pre-order now: Broken-Hearted on Blackpool Sands (mybook.to/BlackpoolSands)

AFTERWORD

Thank you so much for reading the first book in the 'Dreaming of Devon' series. I grew up in Devon and still visit regularly, and it seemed like the perfect place to set a new series. I have another series, 'The South West Series' set in the same area - read on for more information!

I love to read reviews and hear from my readers. You can contact me at rebeccapaulinyi@gmail.com.

BOOKS BY THIS AUTHOR

The Worst Christmas Ever?

Can the magic of the Christmas season be rediscovered in a small Devon town?

When Shirley 'Lee' Jones returns home from an awful day at the office, the last thing she expects to find is her husband in bed with another woman. Six weeks until Christmas, and Lee finds the life she had so carefully planned has been utterly decimated.

Hurt, angry and confused, Lee makes a whirlwind decision to drive her problems away and ends up in Totnes, an eccentric town in the heart of Devon. As Christmas approaches, Lee tries to figure out what path her life will follow now, as she looks at it from the perspective of a soon-to-be 31-year-old divorcée.

Can she ever return to her normal life? Or is a new reality - and a new man - on the horizon?

Finding herself and flirting with the handsome local police officer might just make this the best Christmas ever.

Fans of Jill Mansell and Sophie Kinsella are loving this romantic series.

Buy 'The Worst Christmas Ever?' and begin your journey to Devon today!

Lawyers And Lattes

Feeling The Fireworks

The Best Christmas Ever

Trouble In Tartan

Summer Of Sunshine

Healing The Heartbreak

Dancing Till Dawn

At The Stroke Of Thirty

Life Begins At Thirty

Printed in Great Britain
by Amazon

41995723R00121